CURSE ON THE SEA

Geoffrey Trease was born in 1909, and has always loved writing and history. His first children's novel, *Bows against the Barons*, published in 1934, combined the two. He is now the highly acclaimed author of over one hundred books for children and a number of adult works, including novels and a history of London. He has been published in twenty languages.

Having travelled widely in Europe, lived in Russia and served in India during the Second World War, Geoffrey Trease now lives in Bath, close to his daughter, a college lecturer, and in constant touch with his four granddaughters and his great-grandchildren.

Curse on the Sea

Geoffrey Trease

*Hodder
Children's
Books*

a division of Hodder Headline plc

First published in Great Britain in 1996
by Hodder Children's Books

A Catalogue record for this book is available from
the British Library

ISBN 0 340 63598 3

Typeset by Avon Dataset Ltd, Bidford-on-Avon, Warks

Printed and bound in Great Britain by
Cox & Wyman Ltd, Reading, Berks

Hodder Children's Books
A division of Hodder Headline plc
338 Euston Road
London NW1 3BH

For Elinor

One

'I've been thinking,' Walter said. 'Your girlhood's getting near its end.'

'Oh?' I said. In the cut-throat rivalry of the theatre world it's wise to think before you admit anything. I stared down at him, sprawled on the grass. His eyes were screwed up against the sun.

'Time's slipping by, Rob. You'll find it harder, trying to pass for a girl.'

The awkward truth stabbed me. I knew well enough. But I'd make a joke of it. 'At this moment, maybe. We're not on stage – luckily!'

It had been hot, trudging across the heath. It was only April, so we had not started swimming in the Thames. It still struck too cold, with the tides sweeping in from the sea. But we had been tempted by the Hampstead ponds, so shallow and still, mirrors to the cloudless sky.

Ignoring a milkmaid in the distance we had stripped and plunged in. Now, while we waited for the sun to dry us, no one would have mistaken me for Ophelia.

Walter was not to be put off. 'Be serious. With costume and wigs and padding you can fool an audience. They *know*, of course, but they want to be fooled. And you're clever with the walk. And the way you stand. You can trip across the stage very daintily. No one would guess the size of your feet under the skirt.'

'Thank you.'

'But you can't do anything about your *height*.'

I went cold at that reminder. Almost literally – for I stooped instinctively, grabbed my shirt, and dragged it over my damp shoulders. My height had been worrying me for some time.

It was worse than the breaking of my voice. I'd overcome that – in the theatre. In the church choir, of course, it had finished me as a singing boy. On-stage the change was not so drastic, the requirements not so exacting. After an awkward period one's voice settled down. Some actors went on playing female roles when they were grown men. That would not have appealed to me. But for the present I had cultivated a light quality of voice which I could adapt to either sex.

Height was different. This last year I'd been shooting up like a sapling. That's something you can't disguise. Who wants a Juliet that size, however soft her speech? Or a Desdemona who looks as if she'd hold her own in a strangling match with Othello?

Size was no immediate problem for Walter, though actually he was older than I was. As he was now, sunning himself, stark as Adam, I envied his muscles and maturity. At this rate, we other boys teased him, he would soon have a chest as shaggy as a sheepdog's. But all that could be hidden by his stage costume.

Height couldn't. Inches were inescapable.

By rights, I felt, when one grew out of female roles, one should step into male ones. It was not so simple. There were too many experienced actors ahead of you. You didn't at once exchange Ophelia's part for Hamlet's, or even Horatio's. You might face months of merely carrying a spear.

'You can always count on one part,' said Walter mockingly. 'Witch in *Macbeth*. You needn't stand up straight. Just have to crouch and creep – and croak and cackle! And as you're a Scotsman anyhow—'

They never let me forget that my father had come down with King James thirty years ago – like him, to seek his fortune in England. Mother was a Londoner, I'd been to school at Westminster, I'd never set foot in Scotland or was likely to – but I was a Scot, different from all the other boys. Just right to play a witch on a blasted heath.

At that moment I could have blasted Hampstead. I pulled up my breeches and thrust my big feet into my shoes. 'Come on,' I said sourly. And changed the subject, as we began the long walk to Westminster, to the more general problems of the theatre in summer.

It was always a season of uncertainty, even for the veterans in the company. There was the haunting fear: would there be plague this year, plague bad enough to close the playhouses? That had happened eight years ago, in 1625, King Charles's coronation year, ruining everything. Each year that passed without a major outbreak increased the chance that the next summer the sickness would return.

Even without that, business was usually slack. The nobility went off to their landed estates. The court might go on progress, touring in some district remote from London. It would be harder to fill the more expensive seats. A theatre might even close its doors. Actors might have to become strolling players, visiting small towns, begging permission from mayors and magistrates to set up their stages in market-houses and innyards.

And 1633 might prove to be particularly difficult. The court was going further, and for longer, than usual.

King Charles, like James before him, was King of Scotland as well as of England. He had left Scotland before he was four and, like my father, never returned. Not even for a separate coronation in Edinburgh. Now at last – eight years after coming to the throne – he was going there for the ceremony.

In the theatre this news had caused us all dismay. It would involve so many of our best patrons. A hundred and fifty lords were to make the long journey. They would be away for months.

Just my luck, I thought glumly, when my own future was approaching a crossroads.

Sure enough, that evening, Dad harked back to the subject. 'I blame myself I wasn't firm,' he said at

supper. 'I should have got you a proper apprenticeship.'

'It is a proper apprenticeship,' I said. 'Good as.'

'Not in a real trade. You've no security.'

'Who wants security?'

'You'll learn,' he said dourly.

A proper apprenticeship was to a regular trade. A
blacksmith's or a grocer's or a waterman's, like his
own. By the end of seven years you'd learnt all there
was to know and had a skill for which there was a
steady demand. Your master might take you on
himself, even make you a partner, even – if he had
no sons, Dad said – give you his daughter to wed
and his business to inherit eventually–

I snorted at this point. But Dad went on, unruffled,
'You can't count on that. But you're free to set up
on your own. You'll never starve. You've a real trade
at your fingertips . . .'

'I *shall* have. You'd be surprised at all we're taught.'

Every boy in the company ranked as apprentice to
one actor or another. But I knew what Dad meant
about 'security'. Actors had none themselves.

They were sharers in the profits. If box-office
receipts were low, if the theatre closed, there
were no profits. A year hence there might be no

company. The actor I was under lived in shabby lodgings. He could not provide me with the board and lodging I'd have had from my master in any other trade.

Mr Dyce could only teach me my art. I learned dancing and various acrobatic tricks. I learned songs I'd certainly never have been taught in the church choir. I was trained to stand and speak, to bow or curtsy, to imitate feminine gestures. I was good at fencing, ready for the day when I should have men's parts that required it.

I knew how to die with gruesome realism when stabbed. A stage dagger had a hollow handle, so that the blade slid back into it on impact. You had a bladder full of blood hidden under your doublet. You got it from the butcher's. 'Sheep's blood,' Mr Dyce insisted. 'Ox blood doesn't spurt so well. It's too thick.' If you arched your body right it fairly sprayed out when the blow was struck. The audience loved it.

But such skills were not much needed in ordinary life.

Dad and I broke off our argument. 'I ought to go and see poor Mr Jonson,' I said. 'I've not been round for a week.'

'That would be a Christian act,' said my mother approvingly. 'I've been baking – take him one of my pies.'

Two

Visiting Ben Jonson was not Christian charity but the stimulus I needed just then. He was the most remarkable man I had ever known. Though now long dead, he has never faded in my memory.

He had once acted in our company, like his friend Shakespeare. Ben was no great actor, but he needed the stagecraft to write his plays. He had kept up his links with our company.

In his great days he had known everyone. He was the life and soul of every gathering, first at the Mermaid tavern, then at the Devil in Fleet Street. Friends boasted that they belonged to 'the tribe of Ben'.

I had not known him then. I was a small boy when he suffered his first stroke. His mind remained active enough, he could write and talk as fluently, but his beautiful handwriting had become shaky and he could not get about so well. He depended on friends who came to visit him, dwindling as time passed. He always welcomed me. He liked young people and enjoyed their admiration.

He was a fountain of ideas and startling opinions. I used to come away with my mind *splashed,* so to speak, with the bright spray from that fountain. He set new notions working in my brain.

He lived close to us, near my old school, and his. He had a cottage next to St Margaret's Church. He had been married once, but not happily. His true family were his friends.

That evening I found him in his yard. He was not much to look at. Pot-bellied, pock-marked, swarthy, he seemed even older than his sixty years. He was playing with the fox cub someone had given him for a pet. One of his comedies had a very foxy character: Volpone. I used to feel sorry for his four-legged namesake, cooped up in that cramped space. Yet if Ben had let him go, how long would he have lasted among the dogs of Westminster? Ben talked to him. Often he had no one else.

'Your mother's a good woman, Rob,' he said as he unwrapped the pie.

On his left thumb the ancient brand still showed, grey-white and sinister. T for Tyburn. He had killed a man once in a sword fight, and only narrowly escaped hanging. It had not made him any less quarrelsome. He loved an argument. He would always speak his mind.

That evening I saw he had been writing. His work nowadays was not in much demand. New men were coming along, his illness had pushed him into the background. Tonight, though, his table was strewn with manuscript.

I made a polite enquiry.

'An urgent new commission,' he said. 'From my loyal friend, the Earl of Newcastle.'

'A great nobleman,' I said, impressed.

'And of good judgement in the theatre.'

'I agree, sir.' I explained. 'I was presented to him, once. He came round into the tiring-room after the play. He complimented me – he tweaked my ear and gave me money.'

'He will not tweak *my* ear.' But if he offers you money, I thought, you'll not refuse.

Lord Newcastle, he said, had great estates in Sherwood Forest. In a few weeks, as Lord-Lieutenant of Nottinghamshire, he would have to entertain King

Charles as he travelled north to his Scottish coronation.

'Welbeck,' Ben recalled. 'I'd love to see that place again. I broke *my* journey there once when I paid my own visit to Scotland. Only I travelled in less state. Alone. Walking every mile.'

The Earl was to hold a great banquet at Welbeck Abbey, his principal home. With a masque to follow, which he had commissioned Ben to write.

'His Majesty dearly loves a masque.' There was an edge to Ben's voice. He could write masques with any man, but masques did not give the author the scope that plays did. They were just shows, all music, dancing and spectacle, lavish costumes, elaborate scenery and ingenious effects.

'Painting and carpentry!' he would scoff. His own masques had meant constant battles with the designer Inigo Jones. In the end the Welshman had usually won.

As an actor – well, a boy actor – I sympathised with Ben. Masques gave little scope to the player either. The nobility competed to appear in them unpaid. Sometimes even the King and Queen took leading roles.

What could you do with such illustrious

performers? What could *they* do? Except wear the superb costumes designed for them, walk and dance in a stately manner, and recite long speeches in rhyming couplets?

You could not introduce the sort of action and dialogue that tested real players, so trained actors were merely hired as needed. I had been in masques myself. Once – and I blush to recall it – I had played Cupid in a tight-fitting pale pink costume, suspended from a lofty ceiling, pretending to fly.

Still, knowing how badly Ben needed the money, I was glad for his sake. This entertainment must *be* a masque, a one-night performance to round off the banquet. A play would have been impossible.

Ben rose to the challenge. He was already sketching things out. I was a good listener. He bounced his ideas against me as a boy bounces his football against a wall.

There must be appropriate local references. Sherwood Forest, say. The Earl himself was its Lord Warden.

I made an obvious suggestion. 'Robin Hood perhaps?'

He considered it. 'There *was* a good story. About Maudlin, the witch of Papplewick, a village there. She made trouble for Robin Hood with her spells.'

'People always like witches.' I did not foresee (not being a witch myself) what an alarming part the theme was to play in my own life.

However, Ben veered away from the idea. Years later, he used Maudlin in a pastoral play, *The Sad Shepherd, or A Tale of Robin Hood*.

He decided now to write his masque round a wedding in a forest village, with lots of dancing and buffoonery. The local gentry would enjoy pretending to be country bumpkins.

'They will fall over themselves to act before His Majesty,' Ben prophesied. 'The Byrons of Newstead, the Sitwells of Renishaw, maybe my lord's Cavendish cousins over at Chatsworth!'

The Earl had asked for a literary element. 'He shall have it! We'll have a schoolmaster from Mansfield – who talks of nothing but grammar! And a learned antiquary, the Derby Herald! They can argue together. Very comical.'

I secretly hoped they would not argue too long. Would Ben's famous wit transform this very raw material?

'I must work in a compliment to my lord's horsemanship,' he said. 'He's the best horseman in England.'

'How will you bring in horses? If it's in the banqueting hall?'

'Hobby-horses. They'd raise a laugh.'

His invention ran like a stream in spate. In the Whitehall tilt-yard the Earl had shone among the courtiers in the sport of the quintain. Each rider charged – truly full tilt – at the dummy figure dangling from its beam. He must hit it squarely on its painted nose or between its goggling eyes. If his lance point was badly aimed the beam would spin round and catch him with the full force of a heavy sandbag.

'If only we could have a dummy of Inigo Jones!' said Ben wickedly.

He had quarrelled finally with the Welsh designer two years ago. They would never work together again. Newcastle would commission someone else. He would also be sending to London for a dancing master and someone to arrange the music.

The quintain would fit in admirably. They were often set up at country weddings. The bridegroom in his masque, Stub of Stub Hall, would contend with six bold bachelors and then ride off victorious with his bride.

Not much scope in all this for Ben the poet! But

he would write a song, to be sung during the banquet. The masque would end with an eloquent address to His Majesty, formal and flattering, speeding him on his way to Scotland.

Ben said he had found my comments helpful. 'You are flint to my steel,' he declared. 'You have the heart of the matter in you. You must certainly seek your fortune in the playhouse.'

'Not much hope of that,' I told him gloomily. I repeated my conversation with my father.

He exploded. *He* had never been one to think about security. He had followed his star. And a very zigzag course it had traced across the heavens. It had led him to heights of blazing glory but where (I dared not ask) had it brought him now? In downcast moods he had given me the answer: 'a bed-rid wit'.

Finally I left him and went out into the gathering dusk.

'Come again soon!' he shouted after me.

When I returned a week later the masque was finished.

'And now I've another task – a damnable long letter to my lord with directions on how it's to be performed. In every exact particular.'

How frustrating it must be for him, after always

supervising rehearsals, now that his health made travel impossible! But he shrugged off the problem. 'Sing me a song!' he commanded abruptly.

It would be tactful, I thought, to sing one of his own. I had always loved 'Drink to Me Only with Thine Eyes', so I sang that. He seemed pleased.

'I could write songs in those days! And I can still, like the one for the banquet. I want you to be one of the singers.'

I stared at him, amazed.

'Your voice has settled down. You can't go back to a church choir, but you will do well enough after a banquet.'

'But surely—'

'No "buts", Rob. You will deliver my script to the Earl – with a letter commending you. He has already seen your work in the playhouse. Indeed, you were presented to him. That should help. *I* shall say that you know my wishes, that we've been over every line together. You're competent to speak for me.'

'I'm afraid, sir—'

He cut me short. 'You will be afraid of nothing. You will have my authority. You shall be prompter. There will be the dancing-master and the leader of the musicians. They will drill all these grand ladies and gentlemen in what they have to do – the music and the dance steps will keep them in time. A few real actors will be hired for the main speaking parts. You can't order them about as *I* should, but you're not a fool, you have the playhouse instinct. With tact and subtlety you can, let us say, influence them. You will quote *me*. And – you will hold the prompt copy. With the business written in!'

'It would be wonderful! If the company will release me–'

'Of course it will! With summer coming. With a letter from *me*.'

I began to hope. 'How far is Welbeck?'

'Who knows?' He shrugged. 'A hundred and fifty miles?'

'Halfway to Scotland!'

'No, Scotland is twice as far again. But you are only going to Welbeck.'

'I've grandparents near Edinburgh,' I said thoughtfully. 'Though I've never seen them.'

'Indeed?' He made no comment but swept on. 'The script must be in my lord's hands as soon as possible. I'm to send it to the steward at his London house on Clerkenwell Green. You can take it for me tomorrow, with a note to the steward saying that I wish you to deliver it to my lord in person. He'll arrange your journey. There's a constant coming and going between the two houses.'

I walked home with my head in a whirl. It had all happened so suddenly. Like one of those wonderful transformation scenes devised by Inigo Jones.

Later I wondered if Ben's plan had been quite so impulsive as it seemed.

Three

The Earl of Newcastle had recently built himself a mansion in fashionable Clerkenwell, a mile from the palace.

When I delivered Ben's letter the steward seemed impatient. He was harassed by urgent instructions arriving daily from Welbeck: find this, send that, purchase immediately. His manner changed when he saw that I brought no fresh problem.

'The masque? You have the script? That will be a great relief to his lordship. You are to deliver it yourself? I have only to arrange your journey?'

Two of his upper servants were required at Welbeck. I could go with them. 'All expenses will be defrayed by his lordship,' he assured me.

One by one my worries were being disposed of. To my relief my parents were delighted by my errand.

They hoped it might lead somewhere – preferably away from the uncertain life of the theatre. The manager of our company confirmed, sarcastically, that they could survive without me.

I was only sorry that I should miss the May Day festivities. Especially the Eve, when we young ones went rambling through the woods and fields round the city, gathering foliage to deck the houses. Most of us would stay out to see the dawn. Few parents wasted breath forbidding us.

Walter and I had been hoping that the fine spell would last. 'If the weather's good,' Walter had said slyly, 'maybe there's some who won't be.'

Last year we had got separated. Easy enough in the dark woodland, though, from his smug expression afterwards, I doubted if it had been by accident.

This year I had thought of serving him the same way. One tired of stumbling round in those shrieking, larking gangs. We were past that childishness, growing up. Of late I had noticed a new calculating look in Jill Baker's wicked eyes when they caught mine. And I had wondered . . .

What did it matter now what I had wondered? There would be other May Days, other Jills. But for me there could be only this one masque before the King's majesty at Welbeck.

We started at daybreak. My two companions, Moore and Wheatley, had spent their lives in the Earl's service. Decent, grave fellows – though Wheatley had a pawky sense of humour. They looked askance at my youth but had clearly been told to treat me with respect. My playhouse world was not theirs, but it was one for which his lordship had a strange regard.

We rode post. It was more important to save time than expense, and the hourly change of horses made all the difference. A London boy has little chance to become a practised rider, so I was relieved to find that these men were no more expert. By the second day, I guessed, their seats were as sore as mine.

We followed the Great North Road. If we had continued on it long enough it would have taken us to Edinburgh. But by the afternoon of the third day, after crossing the Trent at Newark, we branched off on a minor road into that legendary Sherwood Ben had recalled so fondly. Jingling along under those outspread oaks I too felt its ancient magic.

Welbeck lay deep in the forest. As I swung myself

stiffly from the saddle, I took in no more than a confused impression of massive buildings and crowding retainers. The place had been an abbey before Henry the Eighth turned out the monks. Later owners had made it a family home. My lord himself had added a new gatehouse, a stable block, and an indoor riding-school.

I already knew of his prowess as a horseman. He must be equally obsessed with building. I had just seen his new London house. That evening, I was told, he was at Bolsover, a few miles away, inspecting the wholesale reconstruction of an ancient castle there.

Meanwhile his secretary took the precious manuscript. His lordship would probably read it tonight, before receiving me tomorrow morning. He sounded a positive volcano of boiling interests and enthusiasms. At least I should not have to meet his questions until I had had a night's sleep.

I devoured (and drank) a stupendous supper. I cannot recall what. Then, thankfully, I was led to a small bedchamber and left alone. I tugged off my dusty clothes and thrust my legs between the cool linen sheets. I still remember the fragrance of that lavender.

Next morning, washed and brushed, shirt changed and shoes gleaming, I was ushered into the Earl's study and made my best bow. His face lit up. It was the same kindly man who had congratulated me in the tiring-room two years ago. A man of moderate height, fresh-faced, with a neat little moustache and pointed beard.

I had expected to stand throughout the conversation but he waved me to a seat. The phrase most often used of him was 'a very fine gentleman'. He would raise his hat to the humblest country-woman when he rode round his estates. He talked easily with anybody, from a learned philosopher like Hobbes, his nephew's tutor at Chatsworth, to an illiterate forester felling a tree. Anyone, indeed, who knew what he was doing. He talked to me because I had come straight from Ben.

He questioned me keenly about Ben's health. They had been friends, he said, for years. He spread the script before him, no more than twenty pages. But, with the music and dances, it would fill the time available.

'I read it last night,' he said, 'and again this morning. With immense pleasure.'

My relief was equally immense. For myself I had

been privately disappointed – but then I was prejudiced against masques. And this one seemed a poor thing compared with some he had written years ago. Still less was it fit to be mentioned in the same breath as his plays, *The Alchemist* or *Volpone* or *Every Man in His Humour*.

For Newcastle though, I quickly realised, Ben could do no wrong. My lord had swallowed all his strict rules and dogmatic opinions. Newcastle had known Shakespeare too, and vastly admired his plays. But when the two writers differed he followed Ben unswervingly.

I had my own ideas, but I did not let them show. I was only Ben's messenger.

'And you are to take part in the song?' he said.

'By your leave, my lord.'

There were to be several singers, personifying various emotions: first a dialogue between Doubt and Love, then a chorus of Affections – Joy, Delight and so on. The music was not yet chosen, so, when my lord waved to a lute lying on the window-seat and murmured, 'Perhaps, my boy, you would be good enough—' I had to show him the quality of my voice by singing something else.

I chose a song of Shakespeare's, from *The Tempest*.

I plucked the strings and began.

> 'Full fathom five thy father lies,
> Of his bones are coral made—'

My lord listened with an approving smile and clapped when I finished. Was it fancy, or did I hear a muted echo of his applause from outside the door?

There was a sudden scuffling and giggling. Then a timid tap. A young girl's face poked in.

'Your pardon, sir! We heard the singing – I did my best to shush them!'

'Come in, all of you. These are my children, Robert. This is Jane. She is ten.'

She actually bobbed to me. To me! Lady Jane Cavendish. 'Eleven now, sir,' she reminded him.

'Of course. Charles is seven, Elizabeth six—' Another bob. 'Henry will soon be three.'

They lined up before us, bursting with curiosity. A lady came sweeping in, dark and attractive.

The Earl stepped to meet her, hands outstretched. 'Come in, sweetheart.' Clearly the Countess. I bowed. She gave me a welcoming smile.

'This is Robert Hardie, my dear, Ben Jonson's young friend.'

They seemed a happy family. Afterwards I learned that they had lost two earlier boys as babies. They were fated to lose two more, and a girl. But no shadows darkened those golden weeks I spent in Sherwood.

Now that I had delivered the script my lord could proceed with the preparations. The musicians, the dancing-master and the designer came up from London, together with several experienced actors. For the lesser parts the youth and beauty of the district pressed forward eagerly. They bowed meekly to the Earl's authority but, when his other duties took him away, they could not be ordered about like hirelings.

Mercifully the music and dancing imposed their own discipline. They gave a general pattern to the performance. It had to keep to its timing and sequence. Some of these high-born young women, knowing my training in London, were not too grand to ask for guidance. The young men were more casual.

Meanwhile the estate carpenters and painters were hard at work under the designer. When the tables were removed after the banquet a temporary stage would be trundled into view, standing four feet above the floor to leave space beneath for trapdoors and other devices. Vast expanses of canvas were painted to represent clouds and forest glades. I had no responsibility for any of this.

With the costumes it was different. A crowd of tailors and seamstresses were cutting and stitching away. Ben had written down precise notes on what the characters should wear and it was my duty to see that these instructions were obeyed.

Stub, the bridegroom, was to wear a doublet of yellow canvas, a green jerkin and hose like a forest ranger, a Monmouth cap with a yellow feather, yellow stockings and shoes – not boots, Ben insisted, because he would have to dance.

Each of the six bachelors contending with him at the quintain must be distinguished by a hood of individual colour.

Ben had let his fancy run when it came to the schoolmaster and the learned antiquary. Master Accidence would display his passion for grammar in a cassock of black buckram, painted down both sides with the parts of speech: noun, pronoun, adverb, preposition, and so on. His hat and hatband, his stockings and sandals, would be labelled with different letters of the alphabet. The Derby Herald would wear a tabard of azure and gules – heraldic jargon for blue and red – and it would be pasted over with old documents, family trees and county records. I wondered how many of the audience would be near enough to appreciate these niceties.

In the middle of this activity came May Day. All the usual celebrations were kept up at Welbeck. My lord loved the old customs, the morris dancing and the maypole. My thoughts strayed to my London friends. Would my acquaintance with Jill Baker have become closer this year in the woodland twilight? No use to speculate.

There were not rehearsals every day. My lord seemed anxious that I should not feel aimless or neglected. He took me with him on his rides around the estate. I think he welcomed my company. If his first-born son had lived, I reckoned, he would have been near my age.

He showed me Clipstone, his favourite stretch of forest. There was a tiny river, alive with darting fish: a haunt of otters. The undergrowth flickered with noiseless deer. We went to Bolsover, where the rebuilding had started in his father's time. Unlike Welbeck, the castle had a superb skyline position on a precipitous ridge, commanding views of the

Derbyshire Peak. He had made a new withdrawing-room, with stone pillars and vaulted ceiling and carved bosses with horses' heads and musical instruments.

As I gazed up admiringly he murmured, 'You are going back to London after the masque?' I hesitated. Was this my chance? He went on, 'Ben said you had grandparents near Edinburgh that you have never seen. He fancied you might have a mind . . .' He paused.

I thought quickly. Amid the distractions at Welbeck I had barely considered my relatives in Scotland. They were shadowy figures. Would they welcome me if I appeared without warning?

Grandfather was a minister of the kirk. A strict man, Dad remembered. Probably stricter now, thirty years older. He had disapproved of my father's rush southwards, like so many other penniless young Scots, to seek his fortune in sinful London.

Dad was already handy with boats – so many plied in and out of Leith. His skills had helped him to break into the tight little world of the Thames watermen. He had found himself a good livelihood. 'But I fear,' he once told me, 'that your grandfather thinks of me as the prodigal son who did *not* come home.'

So I had not built up too many hopes of my Scottish kin. It was more Ben Jonson's memories of Scotland that had fired my imagination.

The Earl was waiting for an answer. 'It was more Ben's idea than mine, my lord,' I said. 'He thinks I should see more of the world. He wrote me a letter of introduction – just in case, he said. To a fine gentleman he stayed with, a poet, William Drummond—'

'Drummond of Hawthornden? Of course, I remember, they became great friends. It would be a fine thing for you!'

'He said if *he'd* walked to Scotland, I could. Being already so far on the way.'

'Why not, indeed? Though if I were going with the King I'd gladly take you in my party. But my duties end at the Yorkshire boundary. Still, if you're set on getting to Edinburgh, I'll see what I can do. Think it over. Tell me before the King arrives.'

I could have told him then. A vague dream had hardened into a determination. Somehow, walk or ride, alone or in company, I would go on this Scottish venture.

Four

Excitement was mounting. The King had left London. In a few days now he would be here.

Luckily Welbeck would not have to lodge his immense entourage of courtiers and court officials, royal servants and guards. They would sleep close by at Worksop Manor, the vast mansion of the Earl of Shrewsbury.

'It was there I saw His Majesty for the first time,' my lord told me with a smile. 'Thirty years ago!'

He himself had been ten, the little Scottish prince only three. Charles had been too delicate to travel the previous year when James hurried south to take the English throne he had just inherited. A gulf of years had divided the two boys then. Now it was a gulf of rank. Charles was too remote to have real friends. But my lord 'enjoyed his favour', and was now obviously hoping to build on it.

'Mother says that my father will ruin himself with this visit,' young Jane told me. 'He is spending *thousands* on this masque and the banquet.'

She was particularly impressed by the new table-cloths and napkins ordered specially from London for the feast. 'They are costing a hundred and sixty pounds,' she said, round-eyed.

I knew from gossip among the servants that my lord was gambling for high stakes. He was hoping for a very high appointment from the King. President of the Council of the North, based in York. If he got that he would govern the northern half of England, with almost royal authority.

His daughter was fascinated by our rehearsals, especially as the great day drew near and the cast began to appear in all those exquisite costumes, shimmering oyster and willow green, saffron and coral pink. Her toes tapped, her whole body swayed to the music of the lutes and violins and cornets. I could guess the yearning in her heart.

Children were often given appropriate small parts. The King himself had once danced in a court masque when he was younger than Jane. I murmured to her father: 'I am sure, my lord, if Ben Jonson had realised what a beautiful young daughter you have . . .'

He looked pleased. 'You think he might have—'

'I feel sure, my lord.'

'Well, ask the dancing-master.'

With that authority I did. It was easy to work a pretty young girl into the wedding scene, and who better than the daughter of the host? The look Jane gave me seemed to guarantee her friendship for life.

The day came. Her father rode off with his Lord-Lieutenant's escort of gentlemen. They met the King at Newark and conducted him to Worksop Manor. Welbeck's hour of glory was at hand.

A detachment of the royal bodyguard arrived to search the banqueting hall and its precincts. King Charles had not his father's morbid fear of assassins but such precautions were routine. When the guests began to gather I recognised illustrious faces I had seen when I performed at Whitehall.

Arundel, Earl Marshal of England, art patron and collector of rarities from Italy . . . sharp-eyed little William Laud, Bishop of London, soon to be Archbishop of Canterbury . . . Sir John Coke, Secretary of State, a narrow-minded old man, as venomous against Catholics as Laud was said to be sympathetic to them . . . slippery Lord Holland, a turncoat when the Civil War came, changing sides as deftly as if he were dancing set figures at a ball . . .

All these, and many others. A fine lot! I can say that now. But then I was awed by their titles, dazzled by their jewels and gold chains.

The King himself I had seen several times. A small man, happier on horseback, it was said, because it disguised his lack of inches. But he had cultivated such an air of dignity that even on foot, with towering courtiers round him, he was impressive. His father had taught him that a king was above criticism. God's chosen, ruling by divine right.

How dull, I thought, forever keeping up that dignity! Courtiers must guard their tongues. No broad humour, no coarse word. This king preferred a stately masque to a play full of violence and passion, belly laughs and double meanings.

There he sat now, in his high place of honour, smiling with restraint, only when graciousness was called for. Otherwise watchful, alert as a fox.

I stood waiting with the other singers, waiting for our cue to step forward. I wondered if he missed Henrietta Maria at this time. With the Queen, at least, he must be able to relax a little.

We got our signal from the leader of the musicians.

We filed forward, stood in line, made our bow. The music struck up. The opening lines were sung by Doubt. Then I came in, answering him:

> 'It is the breath, and soul of everything
> Put forth by Earth, by Nature, and the Spring
> To speak the Welcome, Welcome of the King.'

Doubt replied, and it was my turn again:

> 'When was old Sherwood's head more quaintly curled?
> Or looked the Earth more green upon the world?'

And finally we all joined – Joy, Delight and the other Affections – in a chorus:

> 'Welcome is all our Song, is all our sound . . .'

I think it went well. At a royal banquet how can you be sure? They applauded heartily enough, but what else could they do? They had been splendidly feasted. And there were more delicacies, more good wine to come. In the King's presence decorum and good manners were everything.

Outside, the masquers were gathering, ready costumed. An army of servants stood waiting to move the tables. The designer mustered his mechanics. When the King rose and led the way out into the evening air there would be just sufficient interval to roll the stage into position. While the guests strolled and watched the sun set over the forest the transformation would be achieved.

When Ben dismissed masques as mere paint and carpentry he forgot the lighting – and it was there that half the magic lay. In the playhouse we did not trouble with it. We were usually acting in broad daylight. The playwright's words created dawn or midnight. In masques it was different.

There were screened oil lamps and reflectors, tin cylinders so that the whole scene could be darkened instantly. There were sunken footlights, mirrors, transparencies, all sorts of ingenious devices. That evening the designer had adopted the jewel glasses favoured by Inigo Jones, creating a constellation of brilliance in different hues.

The masque went well. There was plenty of comedy – not perhaps very subtle, but that audience would not have wanted subtlety. The obvious humour, sometimes knockabout, gave them the release of laughter which they needed after all the ceremonial. Master Accidence, the grammarian, and FitzAle, the Derby Herald, were played by experienced comedians, and their constant exchanges held the action together. Their eccentric costumes were applauded at first sight.

The hobby-horses too were an instant success. The tilting at the quintain was just the thing for this audience. As each of the competing bachelors galloped in turn absurdly across the stage a flourish of trumpets was sounded – and their failure was described in a commentary by the schoolmaster or the herald alternately.

And so it went on, these farcical elements varied by the dancing. When, finally, the bridegroom had triumphantly carried off his bride, a 'Gentleman' stepped forward to deliver the closing speech, addressed directly to His Majesty. Fifty-four lines of blank verse, all sugared flattery.

Deafening applause – naturally. Then mercifully the music swelled up, violins and lutes and cornets in glorious harmony. Everything had gone off well, as Ben had meant it to. I was glad for his sake. I hoped it would bring a revival of his fortunes.

I was glad too for my lord's sake.

I was near enough to catch a few words of the conversation as he moved past, escorting the King from the hall.

'The Queen would have enjoyed it.' It was odd to hear the broad Scots in Charles's voice, though he had left his native country so young. But he had always been surrounded by the Scotsmen his father had brought down with him.

'Her absence is our one regret,' said my lord gallantly.

'But perhaps next summer, if we come this way—'

My lord was too polished a courtier to betray his alarm. 'It would be a signal honour, Your Majesty, if I were permitted to present a similar masque for her entertainment.'

They moved on, the great noblemen filing after them. I shuddered to think what the Countess would say if all this expense had to be repeated next year.

Which it was, though I was not there to see. Ben called it *Love's Welcome at Bolsover*, for the new terrace buildings were finished in time for the 1634 masque to be given there – leaving Welbeck free to lodge the King and Queen. The cost to my lord must have been staggering.

At the end of it all he never got the appointment

he wanted. Fate has a cruel sense of humour. It took the Civil War to give my lord his brief hour of glory at York, when the King made him supreme commander of the North of England. And that episode ended, after the Roundhead victory at Marston Moor, with the loss of all his possessions and sixteen years' exile abroad.

All that was mercifully hidden from us that evening at Welbeck.

For me the eventful day was not quite over. I was deciding my next move. I would go on to Edinburgh somehow. I would see Charles crowned King of Scotland in St Giles's. I would seek out my grandparents.

A dry elderly voice quavered behind me. 'You have been pointed out to me as Robert Hardie.'

I turned. The little man spoke with authority. His dress was decent but drab. He was no courtier. 'Yes, sir,' I said.

'Lord Newcastle's secretary has spoken of you. You wish to go with us to Edinburgh? It so happens that I could make use of a lad like you.' He added rather grandly, 'I am Joliffe Lownes, apothecary-in-ordinary to the King.'

I looked suitably impressed.

Though he was in personal attendance upon His Majesty, he explained, his skills were at the disposal of the court. With so many lords on this long journey, some no longer young, there was frequent need of his services. Ointments for aching limbs and minor injuries, soothing draughts to cool fevers or induce sleep, purges . . . 'You can imagine?' I could.

At every overnight halt there were prescriptions to dispense.

Then someone was needed to deliver them, seeking out where Lord This or Sir Somebody That was lodged for the night and collecting the payment.

'You are an actor. I presume you can read?'

'Of course!' I must have sounded rather nettled.

'But not Latin?' he said, to put me in my place.

'Latin too! I was at the Westminster school.'

'It is only for the labels. You will not be required to recite Virgil!'

He would pay for my board and lodging on the journey. No doubt some of the gentlemen would reward me suitably when I delivered the medicaments. When I tired of walking I could sit beside him on the cart.

So, in this humbler capacity, I continued my northward journey.

We made a long procession, upwards of fifty baggage carts, rumbling along behind the noble cavalcade.

I had taken leave of my lord the night before, receiving his thanks and something a little more tangible. I had one more glimpse of him.

He had seen the King safely to the Yorkshire boundary and was riding back. I was trudging along beside the apothecary's cart. I swept off my hat. He glanced down, saw who it was, and smiled. '*Bon voyage*, my boy!' he called warmly.

He was always a very fine gentleman.

Five

Baggage-train was a dull description for that endless convoy. Treasure-train would have been no exaggeration.

All these armed men, the galloping Dragoons and the Yeomen of the Guard, were not solely to protect the King's sacred person. They were to watch over objects of incalculable value: gold and jewels, robes and insignia, church vessels and a silver-gilt banqueting service that had been Queen Elizabeth's. It had complete place settings, Mr Lownes told me, for two hundred and thirty diners.

'Show!' said one of the drivers scornfully at one of our overnight halts. He was drunk and talked more freely than was wise. 'Both sides, Scots and English, set on outdoin' each other!'

The apothecary was more informative, but in

guarded terms. This Scottish journey, he explained to me, was the end of an argument that had been dragging on for five years.

The Scottish parliament complained that Charles had never been separately crowned there, using their own kingdom's ancient regalia. The union of the two countries had never been formally recognised. The Scots were sore and I began to see why. After King James moved down to London he had almost ignored his original subjects. Their own parliament was never consulted. He governed Scotland from a distance by personal decree.

Charles seemed disposed to follow this method. The Scots were indignant. Charles offered them their own coronation – but in London. Why not bring down their own regalia and save him the journey to Edinburgh? But finally he had given way.

The Scots were now determined to put on the most magnificent coronation imaginable. Over the past year Edinburgh had been going through a costly transformation. It would be the background for masques and displays, parades and processions, shows of every sort.

All this I was going to see. When I had first considered this adventure I had never dreamed of the scale on which it would develop.

'But His Majesty will not be outdone,' said Mr Lownes. 'I know him. Who knows a man better than those who attend him when he is ill? If it is a matter of show this king will not be outdone.'

His summing-up agreed with my own impressions of King Charles. His own love of display would make the festivities even more spectacular.

There were about fifty carts and wagons in that column, and maybe twice as many pack-horses. More would join us every day, especially after we passed the Scottish border. Each nobleman riding in the cavalcade behind the King would bring his own baggage, and plenty of it, for all the functions that lay ahead. Fodder for all their horses and for all those in the original party, together with the pack-horses and those drawing the carts – usually three to each vehicle – would strip the country we passed through like a cloud of locusts.

Luckily, said the apothecary, a rigid timetable had been laid down months ago. Even in high summer, with the best-kept road in the kingdom carefully repaired, a baggage-train could move only slowly. Overnight stops had to be chosen accordingly, and everyone concerned must keep to them.

The riders, of course, could have covered far more miles in a day, but they must not get separated from their personal baggage. So, to relieve the tedium, they made detours – held stag hunts, even – and accepted leisurely and lavish hospitality from the towns and great houses along the route.

Mr Lownes had been allocated one of the two dozen carts lent by the Tower of London. Some were packed full of that famous banqueting service in its strong travelling chests. Three carts near ours were assigned to the royal kitchen, another to the confectionery. I was soon on friendly terms with palace servants like John Ferries, the King's master cook, Francis Husthwaite, sergeant of the chandlery, and Hugh Roberts, yeoman of the cellar. Other carts were reserved for the baggage of Lord Holland and the Earl of Arundel and, when he joined us, the Duke of Lennox.

Mr Lownes needed his own cart. It was full of remedies and dispensing equipment – mortar and pestle, strainers and sieves, drug jars and spoons and spatulas – together with all the ointments or their ingredients, the sweet powders and perfumes, candied ginger and marmalade and a hundred other things, some pleasant, some less so. The cart was like an apothecary's shop on wheels. At every halting-place it was sought out by those in discomfort or distress.

'You must widen your horizons, lad,' Ben had told me in his lordly way. The journey was certainly doing that.

They were widening even in the literal sense. I was seeing country utterly different from the southern England in which I had grown up. On our left, far away, the western skyline was of savage hills, so high they were often wreathed in cloud. On our right, after a few days, I saw for the first time in my life the vast expanse of an open sea, dotted with sails.

'Those ships,' said Mr Lownes, 'are coming from Norway or Sweden or maybe Holland.'

We passed through cities like York and Durham, where the cathedral and the castle of the prince-bishop looked down from their precipice on the Wear swirling past below. The Wear was just one of many such rivers we crossed, day after day.

'A lad should go out and see the world,' Ben had said. And I thought I could guess the other kind of horizons he had in mind.

I was learning about men in all their puzzling and amusing variety – their characters, emotions, impulses and opinions – all the diversity which fascinated him as a writer. These fellow-travellers, joking and grumbling and arguing, telling tall stories of their past lives, advancing their absurdly dogmatic theories, were enlarging my understanding of human nature, stretching my mind.

The royal servants had their friendships and enmities like the courtiers who schemed for their own advantage around the King. There was rivalry between one master cook and another, jealousy between a yeoman of the buttery and a yeoman of the pantry, each eager to assert his status. Goodness knows, I had seen plenty of that spirit in the playhouse – even Walter and I had sometimes found ourselves in fierce competition for the same part – but at the finish, in a play, everyone is united in a common purpose, the success of the performance. I doubt if all these royal servants, any more than the noble lords above them, were so united about the coming performance in Edinburgh.

The dignified apothecary kept aloof from these petty cross-currents. Yet even he, I discovered, carried a chip on his shoulder. Physicians had a higher status than apothecaries, who kept shops and until lately had been classed with grocers.

'Yet we may know better what the sick person needs,' Mr Lownes grumbled. 'Because we have a shop we are more likely to see him. These physicians will not bestir themselves to visit him. Sometimes they know far less than I do which drugs will benefit him.'

I sympathised. Some of his concoctions seemed weird but occasionally their effect was wonderful. They were certainly less weird than treatments confidently recommended by the doctors. Dried bats' blood, three spiders hung round the neck to cure ague, a flayed mouse to be eaten as a cure for toothache . . . I would have preferred Mr Lownes and his drugs to any such repellent remedies.

I certainly earned my free passage to Edinburgh. I was busy most evenings, seeking out the inns or great houses where his patients were lodged. I was sure of my welcome. As Mr Lownes had foretold, I seldom left without some small reward slipped into my hand.

Afterwards I ended the day very pleasantly with my companions of the road. The news had got round that I was a player and had sung in the theatre. So, in the taverns, I was in demand and seldom allowed to pay for my own drink. It was not always Ben's lyrics or Shakespeare's that went down best. I had picked up in London some roistering ballads with less delicate language, and these were called for over and over again.

The men had the sense not to press too many drinks upon me. They wanted me on my feet, not under the table, so they passed round the hat. My purse grew heavier than it had been when I left home. That would be useful when it came to the return journey.

It was June now, the coronation fixed for the eighteenth. We passed Berwick. We were in Scotland. The Cheviots fell behind us, the Lammermuir Hills rose in front.

Then, at last, Edinburgh. The castle rose on its precipitous ridge. Other hills were ranged round the city, Arthur's Seat and Salisbury Crags making the silhouette of a gigantic lion. And beyond the city stretched the glitter of the Firth of Forth.

It was there, in the port of Leith, a mile or two beyond Edinburgh, that I should find my unknown grandparents. This would be journey's end. Or would it?

Six

A public coach plied regularly between Edinburgh and Leith – the first such convenient arrangement, I was proudly told, to be devised in Britain. But on such a fine morning, for so short a distance, I saw no point in using it. I would find my own way to my grandfather's. After all those days with the baggage-train the sheer freedom was exhilarating.

Grandfather's parish lay on the east side of the port, where the firth broadened out into the open sea. The saltish tang on the breeze was welcome after the dust of the Great North Road . . . but when I saw the kirk, and reached the gate to the grey stone manse beside it, that tang was overlaid by the fragrance from a vast grey thicket of lavender. It was just coming into flower, with a dozen white butterflies dancing over it.

What a morning it was for noses! At the open kitchen door the lavender was in turn overwhelmed by the delectable smell of baking bread. Before I could raise my hand to knock a voice spoke from behind me.

The broad Lowland speech was that of my father – he never lost it, after all those years in London. So I could understand it, as some of the English hardly could, but I cannot set it down on paper so I will not try. My blood may be half-scots, but my own voice and my ears are London-bred.

'Is it the minister you're seeking, laddie?'

I turned and met the keen eyes of a middle-aged woman, scrawny but pleasant-looking. She held a basket in which she had been collecting eggs.

'If it is,' she went on, before I could answer, 'he's over yonder in the kirk. But he's talking to one of the elders, so if it's not an urgent matter—'

'It can wait, ma'am.'

Her look became keener. 'You'll not be from these parts, I'm thinking? More like an English lad.'

'I *am* English. Well, half.'

She must surely be one of my unknown aunts. I rather hoped so. My father had had some younger sisters.

'You'd best step inside and wait. Have you walked

far?' she asked over her shoulder as she led the way in. 'Do you fancy a bite of my new-baked bread? Boys are always hungry.'

'Please,' I said gratefully. I followed her into the hot shadows. A knife flashed, a crusty hunk, fresh from the oven, was thrust into my eager hand. Explanations could wait for a moment. I sank my teeth into the hot crust.

Someone spoke from the gloom. Another woman. Quavery, but intense.

'It can't be – nay, it *can't* be! I must be wandering in my wits again. But this lad – I could have sworn for a moment – but that's crazy. It's a lifetime ago.' The old woman's voice steadied and strengthened. She managed a wry laugh. 'You're so alike – like he was then. I thought you were my Jamie!'

'My dad's name is James, ma'am. I'm Robert. Robert Hardie.'

'Hardie!' echoed the younger woman. 'The name's right! And you're from England?'

'From London!'

'That I should live to see this day!' cried the old one. She started up and stretched out her arms to hug me. For a full minute it was all excited exclamations and my efforts to explain.

'So *I'm* your Aunty Jeannie!' said the younger one.

'Dad used to tell us about you—'

I wished I had not said 'used'. But the cruel truth was that my father seldom talked nowadays about his early life. When we were little, asking questions about his own brothers and sisters, I had learnt the names of uncles and aunts I had never thought to see. Jeannie and Agnes and Martha, Samuel and – Thomas, was it? And another girl—

Now my grandmother, settled back in her chimney-corner, was starting to question *me*. My father, how was he? And my dear mother? I detected more politeness than affection in that 'dear'. I realised that Mother would never overcome the handicap of being born English. I went on quickly to tell them about Elizabeth and little Lucy, and Chris who was going to follow Dad as a waterman.

'Ay, your dad was always one for the boats,' said my grandmother, 'but why he need go off to London—'

Craft of all kinds sailed in and out of Leith. Dad could have worked on the ferries, crossing the firth to the ports of Fife. 'He could have been a sailor like your Uncle Thomas, who's away now to the Baltic Sea. Or a fisherman. But no! He must be away to England with the other lads.'

Aunty Jeannie was peering through the open door. 'Father is just taking leave of Mr McIntyre. It might be best if I ran to meet him. Prepare him.' She fled.

Gran must have thought I needed preparing too. 'It was a great sorrow to your grandfather at the time,' she whispered. 'He could never forgive . . . but have no fear, it was not your fault.'

I almost said, 'Well, hardly,' but it was no moment for joking.

Dad had never really described *his* father to us. He had just conveyed to us an unforgettable impression of frightening power and majesty – and occasionally paralysing displeasure. I expected the doorway to darken with a lion-headed giant, with blazing eyes and wild white locks. I braced myself.

It was quite a small man who limped into the kitchen. Perhaps he had shrunk with age? I reckoned he must be nearly eighty now. But there was no elderly stoop, so he could never have stood much taller. What hair he had was short and scanty, dull grey like pewter. It was Gran who had the snow-white locks framing her apple cheeks.

He seized my hand and peered closely into my face. My father had been right, anyhow, about the impression of power.

'My grandson! Rab, is it? You are welcome, lad. Your aunty cannot tell me how you came here.'

I kept my explanation short. I spoke of my mission to the Earl of Newcastle, but said nothing about the masque. That was wise. When I spoke of the coronation he exploded, just as my father had described.

'That godless vanity? Waste, wicked waste! Worse than that. Part of the Devil's plan to turn us all into papists!'

It was unfortunate that Ben Jonson's influence had taught me to challenge such dubious statements. Though I blenched I did challenge this remark instinctively.

'Surely, sir – the Queen is Catholic, I know, but she's French – and she isn't here. But King Charles is a loyal supporter of the Church of England—'

'Which he means to take back under the sway of Rome! And the Church of Scotland, too, if we are fools enough to let him!'

This was news to me. It was not the sort of topic the royal servants had discussed over their tankards of ale.

Grandfather swept on in full flow. 'We are to have a bishop of Edinburgh. A *bishop*, lad! St Giles's is to become a cathedral – with an altar and all manner of abominations!'

Coming from London, and Westminster, I could see nothing terrible in this. My grandmother ventured mildly, 'But surely, Alexander—'

'I know what I am talking about, woman! The word has gone round. The ministers and the elders know well what changes are planned. It is this man Laud, the King's evil genius. Soon he will be Archbishop of Canterbury – but England is not enough for him! He will dictate his doctrine to *us*. We shall be dragged back into the old religion, the old superstitions—'

'You will make yourself ill, Alexander. None of this is the fault of poor Rab. It's a sorry welcome for our grandson, after coming all this way.'

Reluctantly the old man paused in his denunciation. 'I will say no more,' he announced generously. But he still had to vent his indignation somehow. 'Why did you not warn us of your coming?' he demanded. 'We could have made proper preparation.'

'We need no preparation.' Gran turned to reassure me. 'There is a bed for you, my dear. We live simply. But you will not go hungry.'

'I could not warn you,' I said apologetically. 'When

I left home there was no certainty that I should get here at all.'

'So I need not ask,' said my grandfather with heavy sarcasm, 'if you bring me any letter from my son?'

'No, sir – but if I *did* get here, I was to give his love to all the family.'

Grandfather snorted.

'Poor Jamie was never one for writing letters,' my grandmother admitted with a sigh.

Aunty Jeannie struck a more cheerful note. 'It will be good to have Robert here. Now we can ask all the questions that have troubled you over the years.' This smoothed over the awkwardness caused by his outburst.

I told them about our home in Westminster. My main concern was to evade too many questions about my own future. I must not provoke another tirade. Some aspects of my London life might not appeal to my grandfather.

I asked questions myself, out of politeness and as a means of defence. My mother and the girls, at least, would be curious about Dad's kin. I memorised names and details, so that I could satisfy them when I went back. Aunty Agnes, married to a ship's chandler on the harbour-front; Uncle Thomas, at sea, bound for Sweden; Uncle Samuel, a dominie teaching at a school in Edinburgh; Martha and Grace, married to decent husbands both in a good way of business. Broods of bairns, names and ages impossible to remember.

Only Jeannie bided at home. 'I help Mother run the house,' she said modestly. Which meant, I found, that she slaved cheerfully from morn till night, taking all responsibility but tactfully convincing Gran that she herself was still fully in control. In any spare moments my aunt would busy herself with distaff and spindle to make a little money. She said, without a hint of irony, 'I've never wed. It's only right I earn my keep.'

It was good to be in a home again after my weeks on the road and at Welbeck, living with strangers. I was glad to accept Gran's insistent invitation that I stay at the manse.

It was a simple life they led. A Scottish minister seemed poorer than an English parson. 'The old king,' said my aunt, 'tried to see that a minister had a stipend he could live on. They say King Charles will try to improve things further. But,' she gave a sad little laugh, 'I know what Father will say. "Bribes to entrap us into papist practices!" '

He will, I thought.

A farmer gave them milk. Another parishioner, owner of a fishing smack, saw to it that they never needed to buy fish in the market. Other people supported the minister with a bag of oatmeal or a basket of apples, a side of bacon or a boiling fowl. They kept a few hens themselves, so there were usually eggs.

I made myself useful, chopping wood and drawing water from the well. Once Grandfather took me on a stately progress round the parish. It was good to see the respect with which everyone greeted him. But I secretly preferred running an errand to Aunt Aggie on the harbourside, which gave me an excuse to look round.

One afternoon I walked up into Edinburgh to see the sights. I admired the castle with its battlements and turrets, perched on its sheer precipices. I shuddered at the Witches' Well below. Scores of wretched creatures had been burnt there down the ages. Some still were. I viewed the church where the coronation was to be held – a massive square tower rose from its centre, surmounted by the so-called 'crown of St Giles', a well-known landmark.

Grandfather remembered the coronation there,

over forty years ago, of James's bride Queen Anne when she came over from Denmark. 'There were sermons in English, French and Latin,' he recalled. 'It lasted all of seven hours.' I groaned inwardly. I was not at all sure that I wanted to witness the coming ceremony, even if I could secure a place, but probably King Charles and Bishop Laud had something shorter in mind. Grandfather, of course, was disapproving of that earlier occasion, not for its length but for the inclusion of what he termed a pagan ritual, the anointing of the queen's head with oil.

From St Giles's I walked down Canongate and what people called the Royal Mile, because it ended at the Palace of Holyrood, where the King was now lodged with all his principal courtiers.

Wherever I went, workmen were preparing for the processions and spectacles that would mark the day. Streets were being railed off, triumphal arches and obelisks erected. In every open space platforms were being set up for musicians and tableaux. Everything was to be on the grandest scale. This was something I understood. Paint and carpentry, maybe, but much more. This would be something to talk about when I got back to London.

But not under my grandfather's roof. I think that even Solomon in all his glory would have met with his disapproval for wicked, wasteful display.

The sabbath came. I followed my grandmother and aunt into the front pew. The kirk was severely bare. No altar. Only, quite literally, the Lord's table. No one knelt. I moved to do so, instinctively, but caught my grandfather's baleful eye. 'No one kneels in *our* kirk,' he reminded me afterwards. 'The King wishes to bring it in with all his other changes. Many folk tell me they will walk ten miles, if need be, to find a kirk where they need not bend the knee. I tell them to have no fear – this will never be a kneeling kirk. I'll have no Romish practices here.'

The lack of music troubled me more. For me it had always been the best part of church-going. All we did here was stand and recite together the metrical version of the psalms. I found it dull.

Grandfather's sermon was not. It was fiery. I give him that. He was an eloquent preacher, his voice powerful even in old age. I could not follow his learned theology – how many could? But his dramatic delivery held me. He could have held a theatre full of people, I told myself admiringly. I should have been unwise to tell *him*.

Afterwards, relaxing over dinner, I made my worst mistake. Aunty Jeannie asked a harmless question about my church-going in London. Naturally I went each Sunday, as everyone was supposed to. But there was no strict check, and people constantly changed churches if some new preacher was said to be good. Until my voice broke I had sung in the choir of a church some distance away. Since then it had been only sensible to attend my own parish church.

In answering my aunt I carelessly revealed this fact. If I had literally let a cat out of a bag, no dog could have matched the ferocity with which my grandfather pounced.

'You sang in a *choir*? In the house of God?'

'Ye-es—' I blenched under his disapproval, but could not deny it. Nor did I want to. I remembered those glorious anthems in which we had sung our hearts out. The music of Byrd and Tallis and Orlando Gibbons—

'You put on vestments?' He almost choked with horror.

'Surplices? All the boys wore them.' I had been proud of my surplice, spotlessly laundered by my mother.

'And your father raised no objection?'

'Should he?'

His eyes rolled. ' "Should he? Should he?" After the way I brought him up? I might have known. He was lost from the moment he took the road to England. If he forgot his own upbringing why should he think of his child's salvation?'

That really stung me. 'My father is a good man,' I said. I forgot restraint. 'If you think I'm damned for singing in a church choir you might as well know that I've sung in a playhouse! And acted in plays!'

There. It was said. He must accept me as I was or disown me. The storm raged till he left to take another service.

That evening I conveniently remembered that Ben had charged me with a message to his friend Drummond if I ever reached Edinburgh. As Laird of Hawthornden Drummond commanded respect even from my grandfather. It seemed to suit everybody that, without further discussion, I should leave tomorrow morning and carry out my errand.

Seven

I set out on that fine Monday morning with even my grandfather's blessing, though his granite expression showed little confidence that the Lord would watch over me with much approval.

I shouldered my pack with most of my few belongings, for it was likely I should be away for a day or two. I remembered from Ben's account of Hawthornden hospitality that Drummond kept up a high standard. And the name of Jonson should open his door to me.

It was only seven or eight miles, mostly by a straight road busy at that hour with country carts heading for Leith or Edinburgh. It was hot and dusty, so I was glad when I reached the North Esk, flowing out of the Pentland hills. A ruined castle, Roslin, looked down from a wooded precipice.

'Hawthornden?' said a man. 'Ay, you turn off here to the left. Follow the river down the glen – there's a path, you'll not go wrong. You'll see the laird's house above you, on a red cliff. A mile or two, no more.'

It was a new world I stepped into. New, as I realised later, in more ways than one.

There were no such wild gorges in the corner of southern England which was all I knew. True, in the past weeks I had travelled the length of the kingdom, but we had followed the Great North Road, so I had never seen a Yorkshire dale. These tangled woodlands clinging to the heights, these soaring trees that roofed over the frothy river and created an eerie green twilight, were something completely fresh.

It was so quiet after the voices and rumbling wheels of the road, so cool out of the sun's glare. I knelt on a slab of rock by the river, cupped my hands, and drank. Then splashed my hot face, humped my pack again, and walked on, much refreshed.

The rough path stuck close to the windings of the river, which I seldom lost sight of for more than a few moments, when there was a dense thicket or a heap of tumbled boulders. Birds sang high overhead, the stream babbled and chuckled, but I heard neither voice nor footstep ahead of me. There was no movement but the shudder of foliage, the flash of tiny foaming cataracts.

Until . . . what was that softer gleam of white between the branches, low over the water?

I froze where I was and stared. I saw it again. Pale, moving with purpose, you might say, not the to-and-fro motion of leaves. Not green, either. White in the shadowy gloom. Suddenly I knew.

It may sound odd, but I was transported back to the schoolroom at Westminster. Who was that beautiful boy in Greek legend, the friend of Hercules? Hylas? His looks had delighted the nymphs of Mysia as they watched him drawing water from a fountain. They had all fallen in love with him. They had carried him off, and he had never been seen again.

That schoolroom memory had been stirred by the flash of a wet white shoulder. But this was Scotland today, not ancient Greece. It could hardly be a nymph. Though (Dad had once told me) some simple country folk still believed in magical water sprites who haunted Highland streams. Nixies. The word had amused me and lingered in my mind.

Hard-headed young Londoners did not believe in such fancies. I did not really suppose there was a nixy down there in the river just ahead of me. I did not flatter myself that I was attractive enough to be kidnapped, anyhow.

It must be an ordinary mortal I had seen. Could it be a girl? Curiosity, if not good manners, told me to steal forward with utmost care.

The Esk broadened out here into a pool, a placid mirror to the overarching trees. It was probably quite deep. The girl – and it was a girl – was up to her waist, though quite near the bank. When she leaned forward a mass of long red-gold hair tumbled over her shoulders. She was looking away from me across the pool. She glistened wet in a stray sunbeam slanting down through the treetops. As she bent, her backbone gleamed like a longbow ready to shoot.

Suddenly, from somewhere near, a dog growled. A low, menacing growl of warning. I stiffened. My raised hand stopped on the branch it was meant to push aside.

The back straightened. The startled girl looked round. 'What is it, Snapper?' she rebuked the invisible dog. Then, in a different voice, realising that the growl might have had good reason: 'Who's there?' Without waiting for an answer she sensibly plunged into the water and became no more than a red-gold head floating in the centre of the pool.

Another growl, more aggressive than the first, suggested that I should be wise to retreat. I did so, stumbling back through the undergrowth to the path. Just as I reached it I stumbled over a hidden rock and flung out a hand to save myself. There was another rock, standing up rough and jagged. I felt the momentary pain of scraped fingers, but for the moment was conscious of nothing more. It was only when I slowed down to get my breath – there being no sign of any pursuing dog – that I found my stocking oozing blood.

'Serve you right,' I muttered. 'The price of wanton wickedness!' After a few days at the manse some of my grandfather's vocabulary had begun to rub off on me.

I sat down at the water's edge and gingerly peeled off my woollen stocking. The force of my fall and the sharpness of the rock edge had gashed the soft flesh of my calf. I had broken no bone but there was a lot of blood.

I bunched up my ruined stocking and mopped off what I could. I had spare stockings in my pack but it was useless to put them on until I could stop the bleeding. Cold water might help. I thrust my foot into the river. Red streaks raced away in the current.

I was cleansing the wound at least. I fumbled in my pack, wondering what I could spare to serve as a bandage.

There was a soft patter along the path. An old sheepdog appeared, paused at sight of me, and turned his head as though for instructions. Was this the hellhound I had fled from?

His mistress came into view. She was decently dressed in country style, her coarse homespun skirt sensibly hitched up for this rough walking, her feet bare, wearing a broad-brimmed hat of straw. The hair escaping from under it was unmistakable.

She stopped short. Then concern overcame her caution.

'Oh, you poor laddie!'

She crouched beside me, thrust her hand into the water and gently fingered my foot and calf. 'Nothing broken,' she announced confidently. I knew that, but it was good to have her opinion. 'But we must stop this bleeding. Were you looking for my grandmother?'

This seemed to me a surprising question. I was not looking for anyone's grandmother. Why should I? This wild ravine was no place to look for grandmothers.

78

'No,' I said. I must frame my answers carefully. I must not reveal that I had seen her before. Her calm manner suggested that she had no suspicion. Probably she had decided by now that the old dog's growl had been a false alarm and that there had never been any stranger near her bathing-pool.

I fancied I had carried off this awkward encounter rather well. It could have been embarrassing for her. I had been skilful enough to spare her that.

Only long afterwards did she confess, with a chuckle, that she had guessed my identity from the first moment she saw me bathing my leg. But I had looked harmless and the sight of the blood had roused her sympathy. So, to save *me* embarrassment, she gave no hint that mine was the face she had seen peering through the undergrowth.

She had no more expected to see me again than I had to meet her. She had to walk along this path because it led to the place where she lived with her grandmother.

'I'm on my way to the laird's house,' I explained.

'*He's* a good man!' she said warmly. She seemed glad to know that I had a respectable reason for being in the glen. 'But you can't go up to the big house like this. My gran will know what's best. Meantime—' She tore a strip from the towel she was carrying and bandaged my leg with skilful fingers.

Soon another little path forked off through the trees to the base of the cliff. It led to the mouth of a cave, screened by dense bushes. There was a scent of wood smoke in the air. The sheepdog trotted forward, a woman's voice croaked a feeble welcome. 'Good dog, Snapper. *Good* dog.'

'Gran knows what's best for cuts,' the girl whispered. 'Everyone hereabouts comes to her. Mother Hume, the wise woman.'

From the way she pronounced those last words I guessed that her grandmother was what people called a white witch. She was wise to mysterious herbal remedies that often worked. Women like that are a godsend in places far from doctors or apothecaries.

We walked forward. The old woman sat in the cave mouth, bent and brown and wrinkled as a walnut. She peered at me with watery blue eyes.

'Who've you brought me, Barbary?'

I had never met this form of the name. I liked it. Softer somehow than 'Barbara'. Like the fingertips that a few minutes ago had been so gentle on my leg.

'Robert Hardie,' she answered. 'His grandfather

is a minister in Leith.' I had told her this much, as we walked along.

Though her grandmother seemed half-blind she clearly knew what she was doing.

She wound off the bandage, studied my outstretched leg, and grunted instructions which sent Barbary running to fetch things from the cave. The bleeding had slackened. She dabbed away, then pressed something soft – moss, I think – along the line of the cut, and smeared on a cool ointment. 'You can bind it up again, dear.' Barbary did so.

I murmured something grateful and complimentary. The girl whispered close in my ear, 'It is all she can do. To earn her daily bread.'

Of course! They must be poor, living here, like this. I took the hint. 'I – I must give you something—'

'People give what they can. But if it's difficult—'

'Oh, no.' I fumbled, then held out my hand with a selection of coins spread in my open palm. 'Please, take whatever is proper.'

She took a small coin and passed it to her grandmother. The old woman squinted at it and remarked discontentedly, 'He talks like an English lad. They are all rich in England.'

'I don't think Robert is rich, Gran.' She made an apologetic face at me.

'I can pay my way,' I assured her and held out my hand again. She picked another coin reluctantly. The old woman grunted approval.

I repeated my appreciation of their kindness. 'I must be going now—'

'I'll show you the way,' said Barbary.

My heart leapt. I forced myself to say, 'I must not trouble you.'

'No trouble. I've some medicine to deliver there. One of the servants is sick.'

I remembered my errands for the apothecary. Barbary must do the same for her grandmother.

'The laird is kind,' she explained as we turned back down the glen. 'He offered Gran a cottage, rent-free. But she won't give up her cave. The glen's a good place for the herbs. Some grow in awkward places, dangerous even. But she's taught me to recognise them, now she can't clamber about as she did once. And there's another good reason for staying in the cave.'

'Yes?'

'It's a private place. Many of the folk who come to her are women, girls too, often younger than me.

They'd sooner walk down the glen than be seen knocking on her door in the village. They don't want to set tongues wagging.'

'I understand.'

We were passing the pool where I had first seen her. 'This is a good place for salmon,' she said casually. But I sensed a slight tension in her. Was she aware of the slight tension I was feeling myself? We passed on down the river. This stretch was fresh to me and held no memories.

She asked how I had come from England, and seemed fascinated by my answers. 'I've never been anywhere,' she said, 'or seen anyone famous. I don't suppose I ever shall.'

All too soon she pointed out Hawthornden, high above us on its red cliff. Its main feature was an ancient-looking tower. We climbed the steep path. At the last turning she held out her hand. 'You had better arrive alone,' she said. Obedient but reluctant, I marched on, up to the door.

Eight

The laird's house was old. Later he rebuilt it, but that day it was still the house in which Ben had stayed years ago. The stone tower, almost a fortress, dated from the age of feuds and forays.

I knocked on the massive iron-bound door. A man asked my business. When I said that I was from London, with a letter for the laird from Ben Jonson, his manner was transformed.

Inside, it was very different from the home of an English country squire. We passed a high vaulted kitchen, thick with savoury smells. Women were busy round the huge arched fireplace. I hoped this meant that the laird had not yet dined. I was suddenly ravenous after my long walk.

We climbed a wide spiral staircase into a hall with white plastered walls and a flagstoned floor. A tall window looked down into a courtyard. Through an open door I caught a glimpse of a great chamber with a painted ceiling, a polished floor, and tapestries of hunting scenes. A young woman sat nursing a baby. The serving man mounted another flight of stairs.

Drummond stood in an open doorway, eyes alight, hand outstretched. Behind him a positive cliff of close-packed bookshelves rose to the ceiling.

'A friend of Ben Jonson's? Come in, come in. You're most welcome. You have a letter from him?' He took it, scanned it eagerly, and exclaimed with relief. 'So, he can write – there is no paralysis.'

I assured him that Ben could not only write but had just composed a masque for the entertainment of the King. He waved me to a seat and poured out questions on Ben's health and circumstances.

He was in his late forties, polished in speech and manner. I knew he had travelled widely abroad and studied law in Paris. His father had been a gentleman usher at the court of King James and he had been to court himself. He was well connected, kinsman to the Earl of Perth, lifelong friend to the new Earl of Stirling.

At twenty-four, I learned afterwards, he had inherited Hawthornden on the death of his father.

He had given up his study of the law and turned to the running of his estate – and to his real interest, which was literature. Hence this book-crammed study with its innumerable volumes in English and French and Italian and other languages. Poetry was his chief passion, not plays: Spenser and Sir Philip Sidney and foreign poets like the Italian Petrarch. It must have been poetry that drew him to Ben. There could hardly have been a greater contrast between two men – the courtly laird and the blunt-spoken ex-bricklayer with the Tyburn brand.

The study had a clock. Its single hand was a fraction past twelve. It was scarcely possible that Drummond had already dined and buried himself again in his books. I hoped for the best. I was finding it difficult to concentrate on his fluent talk.

'What a tragedy, Mr Jonson's illness! Such a man – such learning, such eloquence! When he stayed here I made notes at the end of each day of all he had said—'

That must have kept you busy, I thought. I said what a privilege it had been for anyone of my age to enjoy his friendship. Drummond clearly approved of this.

I heard a clatter of hoofs in the courtyard and a

loud voice under the window. The servant came in.

'Sir Lucius has arrived, sir. My lady says dinner will be served at once.'

'Tell her we have another guest.' He turned to me. 'You would like to wash after your long walk?' He showed me to an adjoining room, then led me down the spiral stairs.

At the table I was cordially greeted by the pleasant-looking young woman I had seen feeding her baby. I knew, fortunately, that although Drummond was not a knight, a laird's wife was known as the lady, and used not his surname but the name of the estate. So she would be Lady Hawthornden.

She motioned me, with a welcoming smile, to the seat on her left. On her right, the place of honour, was a ruddy-cheeked jovial gentleman, Sir Lucius Ballantyne, who lived a few miles away. The other two guests were staying in the house, a cadaverous-looking professor from St Andrews and the head of a Highland clan who had come south for the coronation.

After the plain fare of the manse I enjoyed that meal. The laird carved a magnificent chine of beef and I shall never forget the venison pasty, a dish I had never tasted before. There were green salads from the garden and the first fruits of the season. There was wine as well as ale.

The lady asked polite questions to set me at my ease. About Welbeck, and the far-off world of the London playhouses, and of course my recent journey with the King's entourage. Sir Lucius joined in with questions of his own. The other gentlemen were drawn in. I might be only a youth in my teens but I came from a wider world. I brought a whiff of London, even of Whitehall Palace. I had performed before the King and Queen.

I found myself enjoying more than the mere food and drink, excellent though they were. The lady beamed. She insisted on my staying overnight, several nights indeed. Then it would be the coronation. I should naturally want to go back to Edinburgh for that. The laird, of course, and the other gentlemen, would be deeply involved in the proceedings. Drummond himself had been drafting speeches and composing complimentary verses for some months past. He loved classical elegance and was in his element. Yet, quite unlike my lord at Welbeck, he seemed to have no ambitions to rise in royal favour and win power.

Those days at Hawthornden opened still more new

horizons. There were hours of good talk. Guests came and went, near neighbours and old friends from remote parts of Scotland. Some of their arguments washed over my head, but I listened and picked up what I could.

Not all these gentlemen were enthusiastic about the King's visit. Many criticised the expense. For a year or more every town and village he would pass through had been under orders to repair its roads and bridges and clear away any unsightly buildings. Some places complained that the cost would ruin them.

Some of these hard-drinking, frank-spoken landowners shared my grandfather's distrust of the King's religious changes. They wanted no bishops in Scotland. They were against robed clergy, altars, organs, anything that seemed to them to smack of Rome.

The laird was a staunch loyalist. He supported the King's policies, though he did not like some of the methods used to enforce them. His heart, of course, was really in literature, poetry or prose. Browsing one day among all those books, I picked up one of his own, *The Cypress Grove*, published ten years before. It was a fine essay on the folly of fearing death.

In politics he believed in submitting to authority. 'It is the only logical refuge from democracy.' That word was new to me. 'It comes from Greek,' he said. 'It means government by the people. In practice it would mean government by the mob.' If the conflicts in Scotland ever came to civil war it would end in one man triumphing as a dictator. This squared with what I had learnt about Roman history.

I enjoyed listening to Drummond. Some of his guests I found tedious when they went on and on. They probably wondered why anyone so young should be there at all.

On the third afternoon I slipped out and went for a walk. It seemed tactful and it was a welcome escape. My leg was healing well. The Drummonds knew of my mishap, though not the reason. I was glad to hear how highly they both approved of Mother Hume and her granddaughter.

'It would be a grand thing,' said the laird, 'if every village had a wise woman like that.'

'And Barbary's a fine lass,' said his wife.

'Ay,' he said. But there was a hint of gloom in his tone.

Need I say that I took the path down into the glen?

Should I be lucky and see the girl again? My hopes quickened – maybe even my pulse did – as I drew near that memorable pool. But today the water was unruffled, like green glass, unbroken by a white shoulder or a red head. And no dog growled.

I saw Snapper a few minutes later, for I persevered as far as the path forking off to the cave. He was stretched out, on guard. He growled faintly, inspected me with a sleepy eye, and relaxed again. There was no sign of life from the cave.

Barbary must be out on one of her tasks. Mother Hume was probably asleep. I had no desire to disturb her. I strolled on a little further, drew blank, and returned to Hawthornden.

Next day the jovial Sir Lucius rode over to dinner again and the party grew livelier than ever. The lady excused herself after the meal and retired to feed her baby. The wine went round. The laird was no heavy drinker but he was a conscientious host.

Sir Lucius was inclined to tease me. I doubt if, underneath, he much liked me. Probably, more than anyone, he resented my being there. To emphasise my youth he would address me with exaggerated respect, crediting me with a knowledge and experience of the world that I could not possibly have.

Sometimes he made me feel ridiculous. I came to hate his mockery.

That day, I realised too late, he was determined to make me drunk. While I was answering someone else's question he would lean over stealthily and top up my glass. Once the laird gave him a warning glance and murmured a discouragement.

'Nonsense!' said Sir Lucius. 'He's not a child – are you, Rab?'

I could hardly contradict him.

'A young gentleman must learn to carry his liquor.' He filled up my glass to the brim.

Like a fool I was, for the time being, flattered. I felt I was really being received into this adult world.

After that glass, though, I changed my mind. I was aware of a growing difficulty in following the discussion and in framing clearly any remark I wanted to contribute. In the nick of time I saw his game.

To this day I will swear that I was not drunk. But I was getting so. I saw Sir Lucius's grinning face. I knew what was happening. I stood up, bowed to the laird, and excused myself. I knew I must get out of that room.

I was steady, but I moved with deliberation. I avoided Sir Lucius's slyly outstretched leg, invisible to the laird, designed to trip me. He called out coarsely, 'That's right, lad, go and get rid of some. Plenty more in the bottle.'

I walked straight – perfectly straight – to the door and made my exit with unhurried dignity. I was not going to be sick, though it's easy on such occasions. But my head was splitting. I must get out into the open air.

It was good to step out into the summer afternoon. Again, instinctively, I took the path to the glen. I admit I stumbled once or twice. But it was a very rough path, with loose stones that went bouncing away from under one's feet.

What heaven, though, down in that green cool! If there was no sign of Barbary – and I was not sure that I was in the best state to meet her – I might strip off and dive into that pool myself. That would surely clear my head.

But I had walked barely a hundred yards along the river when I looked up and saw her. She was a good twenty feet above me, spread-eagled across a sheer rock face, working her way over to some cluster of greenery that sprang from a cleft.

I stopped short. She could not, of course, see me – she was pressed against the cliff. She must not hear a sound that would betray my presence. The slightest break in her concentration could bring her hurtling down. I closed my eyes in horror. And in prayer.

Nine

All went well. I heard only the faint clunk of a dislodged pebble falling and the quick gasps of intent breathing. Then someone landed softly in front of me. 'Good!' a voice panted with relief.

I opened my eyes. Barbary was stooping for the plant she must have thrown down to leave both hands free. She straightened up, turned and saw me.

'Rob!' She seemed pleased.

'I was frightened for you. You *can* climb,' I said admiringly, thinking to myself, better than I can. I might have been scared up there, but one doesn't admit such things.

'That herb always grows in awkward places! But Gran has to have it. How's your leg?'

'Healing fast – thanks to her. And you.'

'I've learnt a lot from her.'

'The laird thinks highly of you both. So does the lady.'

'They're very good to us.'

We walked along together. She was keen to know how I was faring at the big house among all those grand people that came to visit there. She laughed at my imitation of Sir Lucius. 'He tried to make a fool of me today. Getting me to drink too much wine.'

'He doesn't seem to have had much success,' she said reassuringly.

'He's only left me with a splitting headache.' A hopeful thought struck me. 'Would your gran have anything for that?'

'Sure to. But–' she hesitated – 'she's not so well herself today. She's very old, you know. She may be asleep.'

'I wouldn't dream of troubling her. It's nothing.' That was untrue. What a fool I'd been, to drink so much! Yesterday I had wanted so much to meet her. This walk through the green shadows by the river would have been wonderful. Now, with my temples throbbing, I found it hard to keep up a sensible conversation.

Snapper was on guard at the cave mouth. His tail wagged lazily in welcome.

'Wait here, Rob. If she's awake I'll make sure I know what to do. But I'm not going to rouse her.'

I sat down on one of the flat rocks. I heard low voices consulting. She came out again.

'It's simple enough, if I do exactly what she says.' I had jumped up, but her hand on my shoulder pressed me down again. She held a pair of scissors. 'I must cut off a lock of your hair.'

'Help yourself!'

'You have fine hair, you know,' she said generously. 'I'll cut it where it won't show.'

'I am singularly free from vanity.'

She burst out laughing, then apologised. 'It's the way you talk!'

'In London I work in the playhouse. Actors use all sorts of words.'

I doubt if she could really imagine a theatre. She complimented me on the way I kept my hair so clean. 'Some people's heads,' she remarked with disgust, 'are like small menageries.'

She laid the tuft carefully on a rock slab and went back into the cave. She returned with a long-handled iron pot, smoke-blackened from the open fire. In a slightly strained tone she said, 'I'm afraid now I must

99

trouble you for a little water.' She thrust the pot into my hand.

'No trouble.' I sprang up. 'The river's near enough.' I turned to go down the path. She laid her hand on my arm.

'No, not from the river. Er – it has to be yours.'

I felt myself flush to the temples. From a doctor it would have been what I expected. It was the first thing they wanted from every patient. They seemed to think it told them everything. But from Barbary the demand came as a shock.

'Oh – of course—' Red-faced I fled into the bushes.

I did not look at her when I came back. I held out the pot and she took it in a matter-of-fact way. Then she picked up the lock of hair and dangled it in her fingers, mumbling some rhyme in such broad Scots that I could not make out a word of it. Finally my hair went ignominiously into the pot, which was placed carefully on the fire.

'We must wait now for it to work,' she said, 'but there is just one other thing I can do.'

'What is that?' I enquired anxiously.

'Sit down again.' I did so. She moved behind me. 'This.'

Her cool hands curved round my temples, pressing

and stroking gently. It was extraordinarily pleasant. My eyes closed of their own accord. That seemed to intensify the pleasure. Her fingers roved over my head, scalp and neck and back to the brows above my shuttered eyelids.

'I hope this will work,' she muttered. In revealing that honest uncertainty she was ignoring (she confessed later) one of her grandmother's golden rules. People needed confidence, certainty. If they sensed that you were in doubt yourself they seldom felt benefit.

The treatment was in fact working. Or at least I was already feeling much better. Was it, as I would have liked to think, the healing magic in her hands? Or had it been – to be honest – that rush of hot blood to my head when I realised the meaning of her request? What I felt fairly sure of was that my improvement owed nothing to the bedraggled lock of hair bubbling away in that grimy pot.

'You truly feel better, Rob?' It was not so much concern for me, I think, as the anxiety of a child to know if the lesson has been learnt correctly.

'Your gran could have done no better,' I assured her. Remembering how poor these people seemed I added in a light tone, but in earnest, 'I must insist on paying you the usual fee.'

This shook her as much as she had shaken me, half an hour earlier. 'No, no! I could not possibly. Gran would never allow me. *I* am not a wise woman. She teaches me, but it will be a long time . . . If I accepted a penny she would make me pay you back.'

A thought occurred to me. 'If I mayn't give you a penny at least I can give you *this*.' I gave her the kiss I had so long wanted to. As she struggled free I said solemnly, 'If you regard that as a fee, just remember that you are bound to return it. I am sure Gran would insist on that.'

She was shaking with laughter now. 'Very well!' Very sketchily she let her lips brush my cheek.

'That's not a proper kiss,' I protested, 'like the one I gave you.'

'It's all you will get, laddie.' I could see she meant it. The hand that had smoothed away my headache could make my head sing again with a powerful slap.

'Barbary—' I began to plead.

'No. One thing leads to another.'

'And what does *that* mean?'

Our eyes met. 'If you're not old enough to know that,' she said, 'you're not old enough for anything.'

That was the end of an exciting afternoon.

Supper that night at the big house was a quiet affair. Sir Lucius and the other neighbours had ridden home. The other house guests had departed to Edinburgh, for they needed lodgings handy for the coronation functions in which they were involved. Those were now only a few days away. Good manners demanded that I too must not impose on the Drummonds' hospitality any longer. Tomorrow I would go back to my grandparents. But I had this last evening alone with my host and hostess, and very pleasant it was.

I knew more now about Drummond's earlier life, though some details I discovered much later. He had not been married before. In his late twenties, by then Laird of Hawthornden, following his father's death, he had been deeply in love with a young woman named Mary Cunningham. Most sadly, she had died just before they could marry. I found, on his bookshelves, the volume of his verses published the following year, enshrining the story of their love.

The tragedy must have been devastating. For a long time he had found it difficult to settle at Hawthornden. For about five years he had been elsewhere, mainly travelling in Europe. It was only about three years since his final return. Barbary had told me of the joy in the parish when folk felt they had a laird again. There had been more joy again when, last year, he had married Elizabeth Logan.

The baby I had seen was destined to be only the first of many. The eventual total was five boys and four girls. No wonder the old house had to be rebuilt and extended.

All this, though, lay in the future. That evening they talked little about themselves. I mentioned my chance meeting with Barbary.

'I'm concerned about that girl,' the laird said. 'She'll never leave her grandmother. But Mother Hume can't live for ever.'

'The poor old thing is far from well,' his wife agreed.

'The girl should be wed now. Or soon. She's ripe for it.'

I liked his word. As if she were fruit. It seemed fitting. Girls are often compared with flowers. But flowers are fragile, and Barbary certainly was not. I saw her as a shining blackberry – with sharp prickles for the unwary.

'It will not be easy,' said Lady Hawthornden.

I tried to sound detached and impersonal. 'I should have thought that many a young man—'

'I would agree,' said the laird. 'But there are difficulties. She has no parents. Even humble folk expect their son's bride to bring something with her. That problem could be overcome. I'd gladly put down a suitable little dowry for her, as I have for other deserving young women in the parish. I feel it's a laird's duty in cases like this.'

'Her father's dead, sir?'

'Probably.'

'He deserves to be!' said the lady with unusual venom.

Drummond gave me a thoughtful look. 'I can speak plainly to you, Rob. In a few weeks you'll be back in London, another world.'

'Anyhow,' said the lady, 'everyone here knows the story.'

It did not seem a story hard to guess. 'She's a love-child?' I suggested.

The laird glanced across at his wife and answered, heavily, 'It would be no great matter if she had been. A love-child is not unusual in these parts. There is gossip, scandal sometimes, but if the young man weds the girl, as he usually does, the trouble dies down—'

'But Barbary was *not* a love-child, you say, sir?' I forgot myself, interrupting the laird like that.

'There was no *love* in it,' said the lady emphatically. 'Only lust!'

The terrible story poured out.

Mother Hume's daughter, the laird remembered, had been a respectable girl. One night, in a dark alley off the harbourside in Leith, she had been set upon by three sailors wild with drink.

'They took her,' said the laird in a bleak, controlled voice. 'One after another they – took her. For their pleasure. And left her there, half-naked and half-dead.'

'Were they ever caught?' I asked, horrified.

'How could they be? She scarcely saw them. She did not even know their nation, she did not know their outlandish speech. There are always foreign ships at Leith. There were two that sailed to different countries only the next morning.'

My horror mounted. 'So Barbary can never know—'

'Who her father was. And the monster himself – may he rot in Hell, and the others with him –' it was not like Drummond to swear with such vehemence – 'none of them could ever have known which was the father of the child! Or, for that matter, that a child had ever been born from their villainy.'

I struggled to take in the full implications of all this.

'You can see,' said Lady Hawthornden gently, 'how it affects Barbary's chances of finding a husband.'

'I'd have thought that what mattered was the sort of girl she is!'

'So it should. But too often it doesn't.'

Barbary's hapless mother had never found a husband. No young man – let alone his parents – wanted a marriage that would start with a baby of such uncertain origins. 'Bad blood will out' was the maxim of farming folk who took care in the mating of their animals. Barbary herself, said the lady, would be faced with just the same difficulty.

'And the bigger the dowry I give her,' said the laird gloomily, 'the more risk of attracting some unscrupulous scoundrel!'

'Her best course,' said the lady, 'is to learn all her grandmother can teach her. As a wise woman, with all those cures and charms, she need never starve. The village will always accept her.'

What an outlook, I thought dismally. The discussion cast a cloud over that otherwise happy evening.

In the morning I shouldered my pack and took

my grateful leave. I declined the offer of a lift on a cart going to Edinburgh. The Drummonds did not press me. They probably guessed I should go back through the glen.

Again I was in luck. Barbary walked along the ravine with me till we reached the highway below Roslin Castle. I took the opportunity to sound her out. She must have picked up so much knowledge from her grandmother, had she ever thought of becoming a white witch herself?

'Please!' She laid a warning finger to her lips. 'Those are words Gran never uses!'

'Why not? It's what we often say in England.'

'Here too. But in Scotland they can be dangerous. Black or white, some folk think that all witches get their powers from the Evil One. "Wise woman" is safer.'

I remembered that Witches' Well below Edinburgh Castle, where women were sometimes put to death. Up here folk believed more strongly in witchcraft. In England there were now few educated people who did. More and more were turning to science to explain the world around them.

As we talked I realised that this was really Barbary's attitude too. She could read and write, but had had little other schooling. Compared with Drummond, product of Edinburgh high school and university, she had no claim to call herself educated.

Yet her interest in the herbs she gathered for Gran, and in their healing properties, was not so different from that of Joliffe Lownes. It was just that her knowledge of cowslip and camomile, of the purple betony she gathered in the damp shade of the ravine, and of the yellow-flowered, pain-killing tormentil that grew on the dry upland pastures – all that knowledge came not from books but from Gran's teaching and her own observation.

'I know which things *work*,' she told me. 'To be honest, though, between ourselves, I'm not so sure with the charms and spells. I wonder if Gran uses them because folk expect it. They mightn't feel they were getting their money's worth if she didn't. She always says if you give them confidence, it helps the cure.'

I laughed. 'Some of the apothecaries work on that principle with their long Latin rigmaroles.'

She swore me to secrecy, then confided an example of Gran's practice.

Farmers would consult Gran when their cows were losing their unborn calves with alarming frequency. Gran would listen, look wise and cast a spell. She would send the man away with an instruction to put a goat in the field with the herd. Within a week or two he would be back, reporting gratefully that no more calves had been aborted.

'But what on earth could a goat—' I began.

'The goat is everything. Gran guesses that the cows are grazing in a field where there's a certain weed, a sort of rye grass. If pregnant cows eat it, they lose their calves.'

'But the *goat*—'

'Eats the weed. Goats eat anything and everything. Nothing upsets them. A goat will clear the field of that weed. While the goat stays the farmer will lose no more calves.'

I was fascinated by this information.

'But you see,' Barbary went on, 'if Gran told the farmer that, he'd never come back to her with that problem again. He'd tell his friends, it would go round the markets, she'd never get another penny for that cure.' She smiled. 'Gran and I have to eat – same as the goat.'

She could justify her grandmother's methods but I guessed that she would have no talent herself for that kind of deception. Barbary would never, in this sense, make a wise woman.

We had come to the Edinburgh road. She tilted her face and we kissed goodbye. When I looked back she waved, turned, and vanished among the trees.

Ten

Luckily I went back to a city full of mounting excitement over the coronation.

I say luckily because I needed distraction. Those days at Hawthornden had unsettled me strangely. Until then, every step of my journey had seemed clear. I had always known what to do next. Welbeck, getting a place in the baggage-train, finding my grandparents, visiting William Drummond . . . but now, after the coronation, what? Back to London, presumably, as always intended. Yet a new, quite unusual, element of indecision had crept into my mind.

Of course, I told myself, I really had no choice. I *must* go home. There was nothing for me here. Even my grandparents were not pressing me to stay. After the first night back at the manse I knew, more clearly than ever, that I should find it impossible to remain long under the same roof as my grandfather.

Over supper Aunt Jeannie asked what my plans were. One reason why I specially liked her was that she treated me as a man, a very *young* man admittedly, but an independent person making his own decisions.

'I suppose I must be thinking of getting home.'

'Suppose?' echoed my grandmother. 'Of course you must! It's where you belong. With your parents. Only natural.'

'Not all sons take that view,' said Grandfather heavily. Even after thirty years he could not forgive. He never referred to my mother. She was of no interest to him. He talked as if my father had brought me into the world with no assistance.

'After the coronation,' I promised them, 'I'll be taking to the road.' Only this new unease had made me hesitate.

To change the subject I described my time at Hawthornden. I was rather selective. It might mellow my grandfather if I told them how some of the gentlemen had criticised the changes the King wanted in the Scottish church. It did – a little. But he could not really see the gentry as allies. They were hard-drinking, foul-mouthed and blasphemous. He only

114

hoped I had not been corrupted by their company. I switched quickly to the laird, his poetry and learning, his culture.

My grandmother and aunt enjoyed hearing about life in the big house, and the graciousness of the lady.

I had meant to say nothing of Barbary and Mother Hume. Unfortunately, in changing my stockings, I exposed the wound on my leg. It was healing fast, I hastily assured them, but at once they were clucking with concern. So the whole story came out, or at least more than was prudent.

Aunty Jeannie examined my leg. 'It's healing well. The old woman knew what she was doing.'

'She's a well-known character round Hawthornden. She's reputed as a wise woman.'

My grandfather snorted. 'Wise woman? Witch, more like. You should beware of such people.'

I flew to Mother Hume's defence. 'A *white* witch, maybe. She does nothing but good. All the village folk turn to her when they're sick. The laird himself says—'

It was no use. As Barbary had said, some people lumped all witches together, white or black. If an old woman had unusual – unnatural – powers, they must

115

come from the Devil. She must have sold him her soul in exchange, said Grandfather.

There was no arguing with him. I changed the subject hastily. I was glad I had said little about Barbary and the way she helped her grandmother.

More than ever I felt that the sooner I left the manse the better. The thought of London became attractive again. With the people of quality returning to the capital the theatres would soon be doing good business. Actors who had spent the summer as strolling players would be back. The less-established, inexperienced men would be competing for vacancies. I needed to be there. For anyone intent on a life in the playhouse there could be no future in Scotland.

London in general drew me. My family, my friends, Ben, Walter . . . Only Jill Baker had faded somewhat in my mind.

Next day I walked up into Edinburgh. The city was already *en fête*, the elaborate street decorations all in place, people crowding in from every corner of the kingdom, not a bed to be found. I should be grateful to be sure of mine at the manse.

Tonight the King would drive up from Holyrood Palace for a state banquet at the castle. All the nobility

116

would be there. The silver-gilt plate from London would be set out, every one of its two hundred and thirty place settings required. This morning, however, His Majesty was wisely relaxing. He had ridden down to Leith, a man told me, and was playing golf on the links.

At the gates of Holyrood I ran into the man I most wanted to see. The royal apothecary was just coming out.

I did not fancy walking four hundred miles back, as Ben had done. I had enough money, earned on the journey up, to use one of the coaches that plied between Edinburgh and London, but then I should arrive home penniless. Why waste my money? Better to double it, by travelling back with Joliffe Lownes.

There was no need to ask. He must have found me useful on the northward journey, for he enquired eagerly if I was willing to assist him again. First though, after the coronation, His Majesty was to go on progress for ten days before leaving for England.

Could my grandparents spare me for that period? I felt sure that my grandfather at least could. I accepted Mr Lownes' suggestion. It would give me a chance to see more of my native country. Stirling, for instance, where there was to be another magnificent banquet, and some of the northerly places I had only glimpsed across the glittering waters of the firth.

It would postpone the day that I must leave Scotland, which I should probably never see again. More particularly, it would postpone the day when I must admit to myself that I should never again meet Barbary. I could not impose on the Drummonds' hospitality by returning to Hawthornden. But at least, if I went on the royal progress, I could delay the facing of the sad reality.

I stayed in Edinburgh till evening. I had a good view of the King when he drove up to the castle in his gold-encrusted coach. He was determined that his Scottish subjects should behold him in his full glory.

The next morning I was back in the crowd lining the sanded streets, under the fluttering flags, to see the procession to St Giles's. More pomp and ceremony. The King was mounted this time – he always looked best in the saddle, and he certainly made a resplendent figure in his satin and ermine. He rode a superb stallion, with a cloth of crimson velvet, embroidered in gold. His very bridle flashed with jewels. I heard later that it had diamonds and emeralds, rubies and oriental pearls.

Behind him rode an escort of dragoons with gleaming helmets. There were Yeomen of the Guard from London. It was all better, I thought, than the English coronation I had seen as a small boy, eight years before.

Then it had been February, with foul weather and even an earthquake tremor in the afternoon. Plague had restricted the programme. The Queen, being a Catholic, had stayed away, refusing to be crowned by a heretic. People had shouted, 'Death to the French papists!' Charles had left Westminster Abbey in tears. There was nothing new in my grandfather's hostility now.

I had not hoped to get into the church but I was suddenly seized by an idea. To have seen the King crowned twice . . . How many would be able to say that?

I had seen an excited gaggle of boys being ushered in through a side-door. If you have been a chorister yourself you are never overawed by a sacred building. It is like an actor's familiarity with the world behind the scenes. Here was an old part I could still play well enough to get past a harassed doorkeeper.

So, while the trumpeters were sounding their

fanfare and all eyes were on His Majesty dismounting at the main door, I made a beeline for that unobtrusive side entrance.

'I'm late! *Please—*' I blurted out in panic-stricken appeal, and the man hustled me inside with no more than a clip on the ear. It did not matter where the vestry was – indeed, it was the one place to avoid. I lost myself quickly in the congregation.

To me, coming from London, there was nothing surprising in the style of the service. The general forms of Anglican ceremony were familiar to me. For that very reason it brought murmurs of shocked disapproval from many of the people round me.

The organ was an unwelcome novelty. 'A chest full of whistles,' muttered one man. His neighbour was offended by the ornate new altar. In the days of the old religion St Giles's had had forty-four altars. The early reformers had cleared them out as heathenish, just as they had thrown the saint's statue into a nearby pond as no more than a pagan idol. Nobody liked all the kneeling, the fine robes, and the surplices. And the principal clergy were *bishops*! The King wanted to bring them back. Scotland did not.

Despite all these murmurings in the body of the church His Majesty was duly crowned King of

Scotland. All went as planned – as planned, no doubt, by his favourite, Bishop Laud. But for my own part, wedged there in the midst of that critical assembly, I was relieved when it was all over.

The crowds were thinning round St Giles's: the cathedral, as they must now learn to call it. The serious-minded walked away, discussing the occasion in troubled voices. The majority were getting down to the real business of the day: the celebration of the great event, whatever it signified and however it would turn out.

Judging by the noise from some of the taverns, I guessed that many had begun that celebration a while ago. I often had to step aside as the lurching revellers zigzagged across the street.

I bought a girdle cake and headed down Canongate, munching as I went. I would follow the great ones down to Holyrood and see all the comings and goings at the palace. After that, to delay the moment when I must return to the manse and listen to Grandfather's disapproving verdict on the day, it would be pleasant to climb the slopes of Arthur's Seat and enjoy the fresh sea air from the firth.

I never got there. For all its fine houses Canongate had its sleazy side. Unsavoury alleys branched off it

– the townsfolk call them wynds or closes – and I had been warned not to wander down them unless I was quite sure where they led. By this time respectable people were indoors, gathering round their dinner tables. Canongate was being taken over by the other sort. Scuffles were beginning. A sensible person would hurry past, looking the other way.

Two of the drunks had just grabbed a lass who was struggling fiercely to free herself. I knew that these wynds were haunted by young women no better than they should be. I must beware of getting mixed up in a brawl. But the terrible story of Barbary's mother flashed into my mind. This girl could be as decent as Barbary's mother.

I forgot caution and ran forward. Then – horror! – the girl's hood slipped back and her loosened hair cascaded over her shoulders. It was red hair. And she was Barbary.

They were dragging her round the corner into the alley. The stockier youth was urging his mate. 'Come on! Once we get there, there'll be nobody. We can—'

The rest was drowned in a scream from Barbary. But that too was lost when a hand was clapped brutally over her lips.

For a few moments the trio vanished sideways into

the alley. When I reached it they had pulled her only another yard or two. She was still putting up a spirited fight.

'Let her go!' I yelled.

The bigger one swung round and faced me, his features aflame with the drink he'd taken, his fists clenched to beat me off. He looked a powerful brute. I could not afford to let him land a blow.

I brought up my knee, hard, where I knew it would hurt most. It obviously did. He let out a bellow of anguish. He fell back a step, his body seemed to fold, his unclenched hands flew to the seat of pain.

His stocky companion still had tight hold of Barbary but her mouth was free. '*Rob!*' she shouted in amazement and relief.

I hadn't long before the bigger one would be back in the fight. 'Let her go!' I repeated in a thunderous voice that would have gripped an audience. 'I'm going to kill *you*,' I promised, putting more confidence into my tone than I felt. An actor learns to convey all sorts of emotion quite different from those he is actually feeling.

I shall never know if my performance would have been good enough. Or if we should have been locked in combat when his companion became fit to join in. He, I am sure, would have been positively murderous by then. I cannot bear to imagine how the fight could have ended. Fortunately I was spared the knowledge.

A new, commanding voice rang out behind me. 'Stop! Take your dirty hands off her!'

A tall grey figure thrust past me, a massive stick raised. The stocky youth saw that the odds were now against him. He fled stumbling down the alley. When I glanced round I saw that his bigger companion had simply vanished.

The stranger enquired gently, 'Are you all right, lassie?'

'Yes. Thank you, sir.'

He looked at me a little more doubtfully. 'And this lad? Is he with you?'

'He is now, sir. I was alone when those two set on me. But, yes – Rob Hardie is a good friend.' She smiled up at him reassuringly. 'He's well known to me. And most respectable.'

I saw now that this soberly clad stranger was a minister, one of the many who had been in St Giles's. But younger and kindlier than most I had seen.

'May I ask where you're bound for now? It's not a good time for a lassie to be out in the streets, even with an escort.' He looked at me now with more approval in his eyes.

We did not resent his questioning. Apart from our gratitude we knew that ministers had a right, by their calling, to question people.

'I'm meeting a farmer and his wife at the Grassmarket,' she said. 'They brought me in this morning and I shall go back in their cart.'

'And you, lad, you'll stay with her till she has found these friends?'

I had never promised anything more gladly.

We thanked him and parted, turning back up Canongate to the Grassmarket, the big open space south of the castle. It was the cattle market. She was to meet the farmer and his wife at a decent little tavern he used when he came into Edinburgh.

It was no wonder I had not instantly recognised her. She was no longer the wild, ragged creature of the glen, though even her attempt at elegance was a little outlandish. I understood this better when I learned that most of her clothes were cast-offs, sometimes gifts from the big house and other families in the neighbourhood, sometimes payments in kind for service. She combined and blended them to suit her fancy. That day she wore a brilliant blue bodice which she had unpicked from a sweeping skirt quite unwearable for life in the glen. She had replaced it with a shorter skirt of jarring colour. She was wearing stockings and shoes made for other feet.

'I didn't know you were coming in for the coronation,' I said, almost accusingly.

'I wasn't sure. But I didn't want to miss it – seeing the King and all the grand people. You don't get a coronation every day.'

'No.'

'But so many things can happen. Gran has not been well. She won't admit it, but—' Barbary sighed, then laughed. 'A wise woman is not supposed to be sick herself.'

I could see that. Patients would lose confidence.

Barbary changed the subject. 'I haven't properly thanked you, Rob. You were wonderful just now.'

'Oh, no.' It was pleasant to have her admiration, but I knew how little I deserved it.

'The way you dealt with that big brute! He doubled up! Where *did* you hit him?'

'It was my knee, actually.' I grinned. 'I got him –' I used one of the more delicate expressions that had been common in the schoolyard – 'in what we used

126

to call "the place where you don't show your mother".'

That set her giggling with glee. 'Serve him right!' she said.

We reached the tavern. No sign of the farmer or his wife. It was a decent house, full of regular customers. So we sat in a corner, swigging small beer and biting into large meat pasties.

She thanked me again for rescuing her. 'I was so terrified.'

'No wonder!'

'It's odd. When I was little I scarce knew what fear was. Gran tells me I feared neither man nor beast.'

I could believe that. I thought of her a few days ago, spread-eagled on the face of that sheer rock, calmly edging her way inch by inch to pluck that herb.

She sipped her beer. 'It's something that happened to my mother. Long ago. Before I was born. She never spoke of it. But after she died, Gran told me everything. As a warning, she said.' She looked away. I could not see her face. 'I – I don't like to talk about it.'

'No need,' I said. I knew it was the terrible story they had told me at Hawthornden.

She asked me more about my life in London. She

knew nothing about playhouses. 'And you mean they don't have women?'

'Not in England. In France, yes. But when a French company came and acted at the Blackfriars their women were hooted and hissed off the stage.'

She had better realise, I thought dejectedly, that if there was nothing in Scotland for me there was nothing in England for her. The London Puritans were not as powerful as the Scottish, but women players would be the last word. The theatres really would be closed.

Mr and Mrs Guthrie came in, saw us, and pushed their way over to join us. I had already met the farmer at the big house, so she had no need to explain me. An hour later I had to wave her goodbye as the cart rumbled off. Again I had that hollow feeling in my heart. I could not hope ever to see her again.

Eleven

I was busy for the next few days, running at the apothecary's beck and call preparing for the royal progress. His Majesty, we heard, was deep in tiresome wrangles with his Scottish subjects, mainly over church matters.

The roads beyond Edinburgh would be bad. A breakdown in our endless convoy could be catastrophic. Everything was meticulously planned and timed, and Charles expected punctuality. Every vehicle must be checked, every scrap of harness inspected, every horseshoe and the fitness of every beast.

It was to be a vastly bigger convoy than the one we had brought from England. The Scottish Privy Council was determined to make an almighty show. It had ordered an extra hundred and thirty carts and another six hundred pack-horses.

This was no concern of mine. An army of grooms and saddlers, blacksmiths and wheelwrights was toiling away under the orders of Lord Balfour of Burleigh. They should guarantee that our cart would rumble safely along. I had to ensure that it was spotless and tidy and stocked with every medicament we might need.

Accidents and ailments had reduced our supplies. Mr Lownes muttered and scowled over his long lists, then sent me hurrying round the Edinburgh apothecaries. Given more time, I could have fetched many of the herbs from a certain cave not far away, but if I had suggested it Mr Lownes would have declined. These apothecaries did not like unqualified rivals.

As it was a dawn start I made my family farewells the day before. I left a few possessions and most of my cash with Aunty Jeannie. Our ten-day programme would bring us back, by way of Leith, on Wednesday week. We should leave for London the following Saturday. So a final call upon my grandfather would be unavoidable.

It might be possible to walk over and see Barbary for one last time. Reason told me that would be foolish. It could do no good. I had no clear idea of her feelings. It might upset her as much as me. I told myself that I would not for the world hurt her. I told myself also (knowing myself only too well) that when the day came I should probably yield to an overwhelming impulse and go. I should be unable to resist the temptation.

July the first came and the convoy began to uncoil westwards in the dawn light.

The route took in half a dozen royal boroughs, or burghs as they were termed up there. They were 'royal' because each contained some old palace or castle where the King could be suitably lodged, while the rest of us were quartered in the town. It must have been a strain on some of those small places: every door seemed to be chalked to mark our various billets.

Our first stop was Linlithgow, where the moated palace looked grim. At Stirling the castle stood on a precipice, as at Edinburgh, over a river, the Forth, rushing down towards the firth of that name. The palace stood in its lower court, a rather weird building with pillars and carved figures. The King's father had spent his boyhood there for safety. James had become King of Scotland when he was only a year old, and his Catholic mother, Mary Queen of Scots, had been forced to abdicate. I could imagine all the plotting that must have gone on. After two nights we moved on to Dunfermline where Charles himself was born.

I was enjoying the tour, seeing so much more than I had dreamt of seeing.

We had been working our way back eastwards. Now the blue expanse of the firth came into view again, Edinburgh itself not so far off, across a stretch of sea. Now we were swinging northwards again, to Falkland.

Another royal palace, with an elegant Italian façade but with round towers flanking the gate, loopholed against possible attackers. Both Mary Queen of Scots and later her son had loved the hunting here. Court life had been brilliant, 'Falkland-bred' the term for a person of polish.

Here there was a sudden change of plan. Charles wanted to see some 'real Highlanders' and headed further north to Perth.

The baggage-train could not possibly cover that distance. But, Mr Lownes insisted, His Majesty must not be separated from his apothecary. So we had to get horses and stuff saddle-bags with remedies for every emergency.

All local gentry had to attend His Majesty, properly dressed and mounted. There were strict orders that 'no rascals, commoners, nor others' were to be allowed in the company. We were hardly rascals but we were certainly not gentry, so we followed the royal cavalcade at a discreet interval.

I enjoyed the ride. I am not sure that Mr Lownes did. That night I found him rummaging distractedly in the saddle-bags.

'Robert! Don't tell me you forgot to pack the ointment?'

'Which ointment, sir?' I could have guessed which.

'For saddle sores,' he said irritably. 'What else?'

Luckily I could lay hands on the jar at once. He did not ask me to apply it for him. Poor Lownes was always keen to preserve his dignity.

I shall always remember that July evening at Perth. There was a great open-air banquet by the Tay. There was music and morris dancing and other dancing I had never seen. Some Highlanders were presented to the King, outlandish figures in strange garments of brightly chequered woollens.

The next day it was back to Falkland. Then we had only to get down to the coast at Burntisland for the ferry-crossing to Leith.

It would be an early start tomorrow, we were warned by the marshals when we reached Falkland. 'The convoy leaves at three o'clock.'

Mr Lownes groaned. 'In heaven's name why? Is it so far?'

'The ferries have to go by the tides. With all the loading and unloading, it takes time.'

I had seen these ferries in Leith harbour. Sizeable craft, that could take tons of cargo below and dozens of vehicles on deck.

The King was taking far more back with him than he had brought. All along the line he had been receiving generous gifts. Two hundred carts and a thousand horses had been requisitioned to carry the baggage to Burntisland.

We, thank goodness, would have no unpacking to do. Our cart, like all the others supplied by the Tower of London, would be dragged aboard just as it was, and roped on the open deck. At Leith fresh horses would be waiting on the quayside.

This would not save us from the same three o'clock start as the others. It was a wild night, still raining when I got up. Sleepily I groped my way out and found our driver by the cart, the horses ready harnessed. A few minutes later the shrouded figure of Mr Lownes stumbled out into the dripping gloom. There were bobbing lanterns and peevish voices on every side.

At least we had shelter in the cart. The cavaliers who would follow later would get their proud plumes shamefully bedraggled.

The sunrise came, a washed-out blur, but luckily the rain stopped. By noon, when we reached the little port, it was a reasonable summer's day.

I could see, seven miles away across the firth, the rooftops of Leith and Edinburgh behind. Further back, paler and blue, the Pentland hills. Somewhere, perched on its cliff, would be Hawthornden.

There was a warship lying out in the roads, too big to enter the harbour of Burntisland. She was the *Dreadnought*, part of the Channel fleet. This afternoon she would carry the King across to Leith in a manner fitting to his dignity.

One of the ferries was coming in to Burntisland. A broad-beamed, roomy vessel, maybe ninety feet from stem to stern, but dwarfed by the man-of-war. There would be time to get a bite to eat on the harbour-front while she disgorged her passengers and unloaded her cargo. After that I must help Mr Lownes when our cart was manhandled aboard.

There were taverns and eating-houses along the quay. Today everywhere was crowded, but I managed to get served. I saw Hugh Roberts, the yeoman of the cellar, and a yeoman of the pantry with him. Their carts travelled just in front of ours.

It was not a place to linger, with so many impatient new arrivals. When I strolled back along the quay the ferry had just come in and people were streaming ashore.

Suddenly, with a gasp, I recognised a face.

Barbary? Yes, unmistakably. But *here*? It seemed an impossible coincidence.

I hurried forward. She turned and saw me. She looked pleased but not, as I was, amazed.

'What are *you* doing here?' I demanded.

'I have an errand,' she said lightly. 'I often have errands. Gran's skills are famous, far and wide.' As I still looked incredulous she added, 'It's the third time this summer I've been over here.'

Gran, in her younger days, had roved the countryside, discreetly slipping into great houses whose owners were too grand to seek her out in her cave. They often sent requests, years afterwards, for some remedy that had given them relief. Servants would bring such messages and, if the medicament

136

was available at once, carry it back with them.

'But quite often it has to be freshly prepared,' Barbary had once explained, 'or she has to send me out to find the herbs. Or the patients – ladies especially – don't want their problems proclaimed to the world. You know how gossip spreads.'

Humbler folk, too, liked to keep their dealings with Mother Hume private. Barbary had to slip to and fro as a confidential go-between. Patients would gladly reward her for her service.

There was no particular mystery about today's errand. It was to an old patient, a merchant's wife on the outskirts of Burntisland.

'It's nothing urgent,' she said. 'Gran said any day this week would have done. But I'd best be on my way, or I'll not be back in time to catch the ferry.'

She tripped away along the harbourside. I stood there for a few moments wondering.

'Any day this week . . .' How lucky she had chosen today! I had not told her it was the day we should be crossing – I had not known myself at our last meeting after the coronation. Had she the gift of second sight? My father had told me some Scots had.

Suddenly I realised what should have struck me at the start. The date of the King's return would by now be common knowledge in Leith and Edinburgh, and the fact that he would be crossing from Burntisland. And where the King went, Mr Lownes and I had to go too.

Mother Hume had said any day would do. Yesterday or tomorrow or— But she had chosen today. Could I flatter myself that she had settled on Wednesday in the hope of meeting me? Or was it – disappointingly – pure chance? I preferred to think that she was merely pretending it was an accident.

Mr Lownes broke in on my speculations with an impatient shout. 'Wake up, Robert! They will be getting our cart aboard!'

Two lines of carts were moving by degrees along the wharf. The local carts halted at one gangway, where practised hands lifted out the baggage and humped it aboard. Then each empty cart rumbled away and the next took its place.

With our London carts the procedure was different. They halted at a different gangway. The horses were taken out of the shafts and led away. The cart itself, with all its heavy load, was cautiously manhandled aboard and moved into position on the open deck, where it was stoutly lashed so that it could not budge.

Everything was done with meticulous care, especially that inch-by-inch transit from wharf to vessel. I held my breath as those brawny men strained and swore.

A slip did not bear thinking about. It would be sufficient calamity if a kitchen cart plunged into the water with all its contents – still worse if it was ours. But what of all those carts containing the banquet plate or the priceless treasures presented to the King?

At last all the carts were safely embarked and secured in rows across the deck. By now, too, the hold was stacked with baggage. We could draw breath and relax, all the royal servants, the sergeant of this and the yeomen of that, not to mention the court apothecary and his young assistant.

More horses, horses of a very different breed, were now clattering over the cobbles. Further along the quay Charles and his courtiers had arrived and were dismounting.

Boats waited in readiness. The *Dreadnought* drew too much water to enter the harbour, so the royal party must all be rowed out to the anchored warship.

By now I was watching anxiously for Barbary's return. Whether her coming was coincidence or calculation, I should be desolated if things now went wrong.

I knew it was planned for the two vessels to leave at the same time. In the tricky waters of the firth sailings depended on the tides. I remembered Shakespeare's line, 'There is a tide in the affairs of men . . .' He could just as well have written 'boys', I thought desperately.

Some quibbling query from Lownes drew me away from my vigil at the bulwarks. Did I think the men had lashed our cart securely? I went over to it, grumbling under my breath. It was so tightly roped that I wondered if it would ever move again. Perhaps he would like me to go round *all* the carts? I did not ask him.

A sudden outburst of angry voices sent me quickly back to the side.

It was Barbary on the quay below, bandying foul-mouthed insults with a seaman who barred her way. Such words I would never have expected to hear from her lips. Others were unknown to me. They sounded Scottish. My father might have known them, but I doubt if he would have taught them to his children. She could only have picked them up from the fishwives in Leith market.

'We can't take another person,' the man repeated doggedly. The ferry was already overloaded. And it was chartered for the household of His Majesty.

She persisted. She must get back tonight to her sick grandmother, she told him.

He had no interest in her sick grandmother.

At this she really lost her temper. 'You call this hulk the *Blessing of Burntisland*? The curse, more like! Curse the lot of you for a pack of heartless devils!'

I had to do something. The man would have taken no notice of a mere lad – least of all one with an English voice. Mr Lownes would not impress him. Perhaps John Ferries would? As the master cook he was the senior among these royal servants. With his belted sword he looked almost a gentleman.

He was standing close by. I appealed to him urgently. 'That young woman – he won't let her come on. She has a grandmother who's ill. I met them both when I stayed with the Laird of Hawthornden—'

Mention of a laird did the trick. Better say nothing about the cave.

Ferries was a good-natured man and I knew he liked me. He walked back down the gangway with dignity, took the seaman by the arm and murmured in his ear. Sulkily the fellow moved aside. A triumphant Barbary ran lightly aboard.

Mr Ferries came back. We both thanked him warmly. He grinned at us in a fatherly way.

'This slip of a girl won't sink the ship,' he said.

It was not the most fortunate of remarks. Oddly enough, in the past few minutes, the look of the day had changed. The blue sky had gone. Ominous clouds were rolling over from the west. I hoped we were not going to have another downpour. The wind was getting up.

The boats carrying the lords out to the warship seemed to be having a rough time. The royal servants were lining the rail and watching anxiously. There could be a tragedy if one of those boats capsized, for the water deepened very quickly offshore. All went well, however. After some tricky manoeuvres the last nobleman scrambled safely aboard and the boats came heading back for the harbour.

Twelve

Barbary had abandoned her role of foul-mouthed fury as she would have dropped a filthy rag once it had served her purpose. We moved away into the lee of the carts. The wind was getting wilder. In the open it had snatched the very words from our lips.

Now we could talk in low voices. 'Is your grandmother really ill?' I asked.

'Not more than usual,' she admitted. 'In any case she always denies it. On Monday I *was* worried. If I'd meant to come yesterday I'd have thought twice. But . . . today was more convenient. And it was *she* who insisted I didn't put it off any longer. So . . .'

'Lucky for me,' I said with feeling.

'Tell me where you've been. Tell me everything.'

She was always hungry for details of the wider world. It tantalised her. She felt it was something she would never see for herself.

The storm grew worse. Men ducked and bowed their heads, clutched at their hats, sought what cover they could find between the carts and carriages. There was no hope of shelter below deck. The hold was crammed with baggage.

The vessel rolled. Ahead of us I could see with screwed-up eyes that even the *Dreadnought* was making heavy weather of it. She was taking in sail, rolling violently as we were. The waves were rising. Fans of spray shot up and came splashing down on us.

'This is the worst stretch,' said Barbary to reassure me. 'The land doesn't shelter us and the water gets deeper. We have to steer clear of Inchkeith. That little island yonder.'

We were swinging round, then slanting off in a new direction, 'tacking against the wind', she said. Rolling more sickeningly than ever. I had not been on the sea before. I could only hope that her confidence was justified and that things would soon improve.

A few minutes later disaster struck.

I heard cries of warning. Panic even. I turned my head and saw that one of the carts had broken free from its lashings. Then, as that side of the vessel rose, and the tilt of the deck changed, the cart began to rumble forward.

I remembered stories of the havoc caused on a warship if a single gun burst free. Gunners would be felled and crushed as it ran to and fro across the deck. In a naval battle a loose cannon with the force of its recoil, was one of the worst calamities.

A loose cart, with its greater bulk, might be even worse.

Men sprang forward to halt it, but they were sent flying. The cart smashed into another facing it in the next rank. When the changing tilt of the vessel sent the first cart trundling backwards, the second began to follow, trailing the snapped cords that had held it.

Behind me Mr Lownes was crying out in horror. Looking round, I saw that this was not due to the imminent danger but to the behaviour of Barbary.

'Have you no *shame*, girl?' he was demanding in scandalised tones.

Her hands were at her waist, struggling with some fastening. A moment later her skirt peeled off and was flapping in the wind. Her thin white shift strained taut against her thighs. Her shoes went flying as she kicked them off.

'Better shamed than drowned!' she said tartly.

The next thing I heard was the roar of the sea in my ears as the vessel went over with an almighty roll.

After an age I came up, coughing, spluttering uncontrollably, as my head shot back into the air and light. I was swimming for dear life. As I blinked my eyes back to clear vision I got a glimpse of tumbled water rising and falling, of faces appearing and disappearing, of empty hats bobbing. There was a vast expanse of canvas spread over the surface like a table-cloth. Then, as though dragged by some giant invisible hand, it was slowly drawn under, yard by yard, until it vanished completely.

Then, close by, I saw Barbary. Thank God, that trailing red hair was unmistakable. Her eyes were open and she was swimming strongly.

So she *could* swim, really swim! So few women could. Not so many men, come to that. Many of my father's fellow watermen on the Thames could not. I had not known till now that she could even swim the breadth of that salmon pool in the Esk. Clearly she could. She saw me and shouted something.

I could believe, when we discussed the matter afterwards, that she saved my life. As she told me with a wry smile – when smiling was possible again –

'You were striking out so *powerfully*. But unfortunately you were heading in the wrong direction. Making for Leith! I could never have caught up with you.'

'Do you think I wouldn't have looked round for you?' I asked indignantly. But in those first awful moments God knows what might have happened.

The ferry must have been shockingly overloaded anyhow. The loose carts had – almost literally – tipped the scales. The sea must have flooded in. With that one irresistible roll the vessel had gone under. And unlike ourselves it had never surfaced again.

I saw no sign of poor old Lownes, no sign indeed of anyone else in the water near us. We could only strive to save ourselves.

'The shore—' gasped Barbary. 'It's not – so far—'

It could not be. Would she manage the distance? I felt I could myself, probably. My boyhood swimming in the Thames had been good training for this. Several boating mishaps had taught me that I could cope with the encumbrance of being fully clad. But if Barbary got into difficulties? I could only pray that I should find the extra strength to help her.

The storm had passed as suddenly as it had broken over us. People said afterwards that it lasted barely half an hour from start to finish. When we rose on a wave we got a brief glimpse of the green Fifeshire coast. It was bathed in sunshine.

I had long ago kicked off my shoes. I was conscious mainly of a leaden weight around my middle. Of course! Not lead, but silver – the coins I had accumulated for services rendered in the past ten days. Not a vast amount, but at that moment it felt damnably heavy. Not worth dying for, but . . . If I felt the slightest doubt about reaching land, and Barbary with me, I should have to unbuckle that belt and let it slide sadly down into the depths.

I was never required to make that decision. We swam on for another minute or two, the shore still uncomfortably distant, when a voice hailed us from behind, bidding us hang on, help was at hand. The creeping shadow of a vessel blotted out the sun. There were voices overhead, brawny arms reaching down to haul us up out of the water.

We had been rescued by one of the many little coasting craft that ply along the firth, carrying goods and passengers between the different towns. This one had come from Kirkcaldy, hugging the Fifeshire shore and escaping the worst of the storm.

They had seen our disaster with incredulous horror. At one moment the ferry had been rising and falling and lurching under the impact of wind and wave. Suddenly it had tilted over – and the mast had never come slanting up again. In another instant the whole vessel had turned over and disappeared from view.

Two kindly passengers, a mother and daughter, had now taken Barbary into their care. The poor girl must have been stark naked under that flimsy shift that clung to her. They screened her from the rest of us and when I caught my next glimpse of her she was muffled in a long plaid.

I was pulling my own shirt over my head, and trying to answer the men's questions, when the younger woman stepped across with a friendly smile. She wore a wedding ring but could not have been many years older than Barbary.

'We are getting off at Burntisland,' she said, 'but the boat will bide there a while to unload some goods. Our house is only a short step. I have a dress I can fetch that I am sure would fit your sister –' she dropped her eyes – 'better than it will soon fit *me*.' She laughed, seeing my big bare feet. 'I fear I've no shoes that I can offer *you*!'

I thanked her. She was startled and intrigued by my London speech. I felt I had better explain.

'She's not my sister,' I said. 'But I know her – and her mother,' I added, to indicate my respectability. 'We met quite by chance on the quay.' I still had secret hopes that it had not been by chance. 'I shall see her safely to her home,' I promised.

'I'll tell my mother. She'll be relieved.'

She went back to them. I sat in the hot sun, stripped to the waist, my clothes spread to dry.

People continued to ply me with questions. I told them what I could. There had been about thirty people on board, many of them servants of the royal household. The capsizing had been so instantaneous, I had not seen what happened to the others. Pray God some of them had been picked up by other boats. Privately I had no great hopes.

It had been an extraordinary thing, this storm, so sudden and so violent, coming on a fine summer's day. There had been many shipwrecks in the firth, but no one recalled an occasion like this.

What a merciful escape for His Majesty! They had seen in the distance that, after some difficulty, the *Dreadnought* had made harbour safely at Leith.

We were now safely back ourselves in port at Burntisland. The women stepped carefully ashore, turned and waved. 'I'll be as quick as I can,' the young one promised.

Barbary was still shaken by her experience. 'Don't leave me,' she begged. She was clearly afraid that I might follow them out of good manners, to save the girl the walk back. She need not have worried. Far better, I thought, to get quickly back to Leith even as we were, barely decent, than risk being separated again.

The boatmen busied themselves unloading cargo and stowing fresh goods aboard. They were in no great hurry. The shallow draught of their craft made them independent of the tides. They could break off to gossip with bystanders, exchanging impressions and opinions of the tragedy.

So the young woman was back before we could grow anxious. She brought an armful of clothes for Barbary, who decided to wait till we were out of the staring gaze of the quayside idlers before she changed into them. For me the girl had found only an old shirt, threadbare but clean and dry, and a well-worn pair of her father's boots. They were over-big on my feet but better than nothing for the short walk to my grandparents'. I was not used to walking barefoot as Barbary did in the glen. Thank goodness, I thought, for the spare clothing I had left at the manse.

I offered payment but our good Samaritan refused. Within a few minutes we were waving goodbye again as our sail went up and we crept out of Burntisland for the second time.

There were no sympathetic women now and there was little privacy. I could only post myself with my back to Barbary and screen her as best I could while she dressed. Then I walked over to one of the boatmen and asked what news he had managed to pick up while we were alongside the quay.

'Not much, lad. Two bodies have been washed up on the beach. Not a breath of life in either o' them. One was a biggish fellow, wearing a sword. They say he had a deal o' money on him.'

That must have been John Ferries, the master cook. I felt a pang of grief, remembering his kindness in getting Barbary aboard. I wondered about poor Mr Lownes. What chance would he have had?

'You said there were above thirty of you?' asked the boatman.

'I reckon so.'

'Then God help the rest o' them.'

Another of the crew joined us. 'Someone said there was a bold lass wi' red hair. She was standin' on the quay, damnin' an' blastin' because the ferryman wouldna' let her on.' He stared oddly at Barbary as she walked over to join me.

'But *you* were *on* the ferry, weren't you, lass?' said the first man kindly.

'I was,' she said with feeling.

'Then you're lucky to be here now!'

'You may call it luck,' said the second man. He seemed inclined to be disagreeable.

I went to her rescue. 'She can swim,' I said admiringly, explaining her escape.

'I've never been afraid of the water,' said Barbary.

'You wouldna' be, would you?' he said darkly. He gave her another odd look and, as he turned away, I could have sworn he crossed himself. Maybe he was one of the old religion.

Thirteen

We had a warm welcome from my grandmother and
Aunty Jeannie when we reached the manse. They
were vastly relieved to see me safe.

News of the disaster had already spread, mingled
with understandable relief at the King's arrival in the
Dreadnought. As the ferry had been a Burntisland
vessel there had been no Leith men in the crew and
it was assumed that most of the others aboard would
be unknown Englishmen in the royal service.

Only my grandmother and aunt realised that I
should be among them. I was welcomed almost as if
back from the dead, and Barbary had no cause to
complain of the warmth with which they received
her.

'Poor lassie,' cried my aunt. 'Sit you down here.'

She had been baking. The oven had not cooled.

Barbary was given a seat beside it. I slipped away to the attic for my bundle, changed quickly and came back to spread my damp clothes on the hot stonework.

Barbary was chattering happily in answer to Gran's questions. She had identified herself as Mother Hume's granddaughter, the girl who had helped me when I gashed my leg. She had even told them of her home in the cave.

My aunt paused as she set out the supper. 'You'll no' go back there tonight? All that way? After what you've been through! You need a warm bed, a good night's sleep—'

'But my gran may fret—'

'Will she *hear* o' the wreck? Up there?'

To be honest Barbary did not think she would. Mother Hume did not stir far these days. Unless someone came to the cave late in the day she was unlikely to get word of the disaster. When Barbary went on such distant errands, especially across the firth, she had sometimes to be away overnight.

Grandfather appeared just in time to say grace for our supper, which as always at the manse was plain but plentiful. Barbary was as ready for it as I was. We attacked it with zest.

Grandfather was full of the shipwreck. He was inclined to think that the sudden, unseasonable tempest was the Almighty's warning against the vanities of the court. He developed this theory with the eloquence of a sermon.

It was not until the end of the meal that he grasped who Barbary was. His manner cooled abruptly.

'You are Mother Hume's granddaughter? The witch at Hawthornden?'

'Mother Hume, yes, sir. But – people call her the wise woman.'

'I would call her what she is. A witch!'

'But *white*, sir,' Barbary conceded.

He was off on his old hobby-horse. 'There is no white or black about it. If she claims powers beyond what is natural—'

'She knows about illnesses,' Barbary protested. She was the only person I have ever known to stand up to my grandfather. 'She has learnt the properties of herbs. And berries and mosses. Ask Rob how quickly his leg healed after she treated it.'

'And very grateful I was,' I said loyally.

He was not impressed. 'If she has powers that others lack she must get them from somewhere. And I tell you, it is from the Devil.'

'*No!*' she said furiously.

Gran interfered gently to defend her. 'Let the poor lass be,' she pleaded. 'She was near drowned when that ferry sank.'

He turned on Gran now. 'And why was she not? Tell me that. They say in the town everyone else was lost. Why is *she* here, safe and sound? I will tell you – because it is well known that witches do not drown!'

'What does that prove?' I demanded. 'I did not drown. Am *I* a witch?'

He ignored me. 'She comes from a witch's brood. I'll not harbour her under my roof.'

'Can she not stay tonight?' said my aunt. 'She's exhausted. I've made up a bed for her—'

'Not in this house! Never!'

'Grandad,' I said, 'it's only Christian charity.'

Now I got the full force of his glare. 'Don't presume to teach *me* what is Christian charity. What does the Bible say? "Thou shalt not suffer a witch to live." *Exodus* twenty-two, verse eighteen.' It really was as though he were in his pulpit.

Barbary rose to her feet and looked him straight in the eye. 'Then I had better go. Before you feel you are obliged to burn me.'

'You can't go tonight,' wailed Gran.

'Not like this,' said Aunty Jeannie. 'Not all that way. It's getting dark.'

'Best time for witches,' said the girl. Even at this moment impudence tinged her anger. 'No doubt the minister thinks I can fly. But thanks to your kindness I'm rested now. I can walk. Like a Christian – almost!'

'Oh, no, child,' cried Gran in despair, 'you can't go like this—'

'I must, ma'am. The master of the house demands it.' Again that hint of mischief. ' "Render unto Caesar." Even I can quote the scriptures. Though I don't know chapter and verse.'

'I'll see her home, Gran,' I promised.

'But even you shouldn't walk there and back tonight after this terrible day you've had—'

'He can sleep in our cave,' said Barbary.

'I don't know *what* to say,' said Gran miserably.

My grandfather did, of course. He could always be relied upon to fill any awkward silences. His flow of doctrine and denunciation continued while I went upstairs and fetched my pack. My damp clothes had dried on the oven. Barbary, in a matter-of-fact manner, was folding them neatly for me. My aunt slipped me the jingling bag in which she had been keeping my money.

With my own spare shoes on my feet now, in place of the pair given me by the kind young woman at Burntisland, I felt more ready for the road.

Grandfather glowered over our farewells. In my fury I could have wished they were final. But of course I should be back there tomorrow. I forced myself to grunt a sullen goodbye as I followed Barbary through the door. 'I was sore tempted,' she confessed to me afterwards, 'to say to him, "Devil take you!" '

By then I could laugh again. 'It would have been in character,' I said, 'and confirmed his worst suspicions of you.'

'But your grandmother and aunt had been so kind. I wouldn't for the world.'

The dusk gathered round us. A sickle moon hung silver over the hills in front.

'We really do have a bed you can sleep on,' she reassured me. 'A sort of bed.'

This surprised me. I had never taken a single step inside the cavern. I could hardly imagine its furnishings.

'You do sometimes have guests?'

'Never. Neither of this world nor any other! But sometimes a sick person needs to lie down after the walk through the glen. Or – with some complaints, you can imagine – Gran has to examine them.'

'Naturally.' I did not look forward to sleeping on this 'sort of bed' after such a variety of afflicted occupants. There would be no lavender-scented sheets, I felt sure.

The moon climbed higher. We trudged on, talking in low voices. 'I loved your grandmother,' she said. 'And your Aunty Jeannie. They were so kind. It must be wonderful to have a family.'

'And my true family is in London.' I told her about them all. 'But *you* have a gran,' I said.

'Yes–'

'And Snapper!'

'But he's getting so old too.'

It seemed better to get off that subject.

To make her laugh I told her stories of the playhouse: and how the recognised way into that world was to be a pretty boy who could pretend to be a girl – and had a good memory for verse. I told her the tale of *Romeo and Juliet*. She had never of course seen a play. I doubt if she had ever read a book. She was a wonderful listener.

I found myself feeling unexpectedly grateful to my grandfather. Without his unyielding dogmatic principles I should never have had this unforgettable walk with her. I scarcely had time to wonder what welcome I could expect from *her* grandparent. Would Mother Hume refuse me overnight shelter in her cave? Never mind. She could not prevent my stretching out under the bushes near by. Whatever the discomfort, whatever the unsettling excitements of the day, I should sleep happy.

At last we reached the turning into the glen. It was very dark. That sickle moon could not cut through the black mass of overhanging foliage.

We could not walk abreast now. 'I'll go first,' she said. 'I know the path. My *feet* know it. Every hump, every jagged rock. You must not hurt your leg again.' Our hands touched only when she paused and turned, and reached out to steer me past some invisible obstacle. 'Nearly there,' she whispered. 'Any moment now, Snapper will hear us and growl.'

But it was not the old dog that challenged us. It was a voice from the cave entrance. The voice of a man.

Fourteen

Barbary clutched my hand. Her voice was strained but steady. 'Who is it?'

'Only me, lass. Where in God's name have you been?'

'Mr Guthrie!' It was the farmer who had brought her into Edinburgh on the coronation day. For a moment she seemed reassured. Then she added apprehensively, 'Is something wrong?'

He came out of the cave, a lantern held high. 'You'd best come and sit down, lass. It's sad news.'

He put a hand on her shoulder and steered her inside. In the wavering yellow light I saw the interior for the first time. Pots and pans, firewood, the rough couch for patients and, further back, two beds, left and right. Both empty.

Of Gran and the old sheepdog there was no sign.

'What's happened?' Barbary's voice was choked with fear. 'It's not – Gran?'

'I fear it is. God rest her soul.'

'Oh, *Gran*!' The cry was piteous. 'And I was across the firth! At Burntisland.'

'So that's where you were? Nobody knew. I said I'd wait here till you came home. I could not think *where* you were.'

'She sent me. I should not have gone. But she seemed well enough this morning—'

'You could have done naught, lass.'

'Who found her?'

'A woman came with some trouble – a while after noon it was. She thought your gran was sleeping, she looked so peaceful. But there was no life in her, no life at all. The dog was whimpering—'

'Where *is* poor Snapper?'

'He would not leave her—'

'Of course not!'

The woman had hurried up to the big house. The laird himself had come down. Mother Hume must not be left there, he ordered. So she had been carried up to the big house, Snapper following the bearers, tail between his legs, whining miserably.

'When they told me,' said Mr Guthrie, 'I thought

straight of you. You'd be frantic if you came back and found her gone. I said I'd bide here and break the news to you. But the hours passed, and the hours passed. I knew not *what* to think.'

'I'm so sorry.' Her penitence was desperate.

'No call to be. I'll allow, for a moment just now, when I heard two voices, and one a lad's, I did you an injustice. I began to wonder—'

'Rob was only taking care of me, as he did that other day. We'd been in the shipwreck. Have you heard about that?'

He gasped. 'You were in *that*? But of course! You'd be coming back from Burntisland. I heard, yes, but none of us dreamt you'd be in it. Your gran had pushed everything else out of our minds.'

'Of course.' She squeezed his hand. It was his turn to be comforted.

'Can you manage one more mile?' he enquired anxiously. 'The laird said to take you up to the big house for the night. You must not stay here.'

'Of course not.' She stood up. 'I must go to Gran.'

He turned to me. 'You too, lad.' He remembered I had been Drummond's guest only a week or two before.

So the three of us walked down the glen, our weary

footsteps guided by his bobbing lantern, and climbed the steep path to Hawthornden.

The porter greeted us with obvious relief. We meant the end of his long vigil. He took us up to the laird who was reading by candlelight. He jumped up, all sympathy, seizing both Barbary's hands in his. My eyes fell to the open book. Typically he had been calming his mind with Italian poetry. The sonnets of Petrarch.

'A sad day for us all,' he told Barbary, 'and for you, my dear, a great loss indeed.'

Lady Hawthornden appeared in her nightgown, murmuring consolation. After a few minutes she led Barbary away and I saw neither of them again until the following morning.

Guthrie was warmly thanked and took his leave after accepting a glass of wine. Alone with Drummond I explained how I came to be with Barbary. He questioned me eagerly about the shipwreck.

'It's the strangest thing,' he said. 'Such a sudden tempest. With no warning. At this time of year.'

He wanted to ask about other aspects of the royal progress – partly, I guessed, to take my mind off the death of the old woman. But he must have seen that

I was swaying in my seat. To me it was the room that seemed to be swaying, along with the little tongues of candle flame.

I remembered that three o'clock start from Falkland. Could it really have been only today? Well, yesterday, since it was now past midnight. But so much had happened it seemed like a week.

'Come, lad,' he said suddenly. 'That is enough for now.' I remember only dimly how he led me to another room and, I suppose, helped me out of my clothes, and then stole soft-footed away, taking the candle with him.

It was no wonder that Barbary and I slept late.

When I saw the laird again the latest news of the ferry disaster had been brought up from Leith market. The vessel had sunk in deep water. As we already knew, two bodies had been washed up on the shore near Burntisland. Most would have been swept out to sea on the ebb tide. If there were any other survivors it would be known before too long.

I knew in my heart that Mr Lownes must have died with the rest. He would not be taking the road for London on Saturday. His cart too would be lying on the bottom of the sea. So I myself would not be starting southwards with the King. There was no longer a place for me in the royal convoy. I must make my own way home. My immediate future was almost as uncertain as poor Barbary's.

She was to stay for the present at the big house. When she had recovered from her loss she would no doubt make herself useful there.

'You will stay too, Robert, until after the funeral?' Lady Hawthornden asked me. I accepted gratefully. I had no need to go back to Edinburgh if Lownes had not survived. I had no wish to return to my grandfather's.

The funeral anyhow was tomorrow. The laird had taken over all the arrangements. Mother Hume might otherwise have been laid in a pauper's grave. Drummond would see that she had a decent burial. But it must be on Friday, tomorrow, for on Saturday morning he was summoned, with all the other gentry of the district, to parade well mounted and well clad to escort His Majesty on the first stage of his southward journey.

'It will be a comfort to the lass to have you here,' Lady Hawthornden assured me. 'You have been through so much together in these past weeks. Those ruffians in the Canongate and then this shipwreck! She tells me you saved her life.'

'She saved herself. She was swimming like an otter. I think I was more afraid than she was.'

'You could not have shown it then. She says she would have given up if you had not been there beside her in the water.'

'Remember,' said the laird. 'She has never had a family. Never knew a father, lost her mother early. I am sure she thinks of you now almost as a brother – the brother she never had.'

Sad though these reflections were, I observed a smile, a rather private sort of smile, on his wife's face. Lady Hawthornden was, of course, much younger than the laird. She was closer indeed to my own generation.

The funeral was at the parish church at Laswade, a mile or two away. It was remarkable how many people were there, folk of the humbler sort, grateful often for some help Mother Hume had given them many years before. Barbary was clearly touched when they paused to mutter words of sympathy. Gran was going to be missed in this community.

Barbary's temporary status as a guest at the big house was accepted good-naturedly by the servants. Many of them too had cause to remember Mother Hume's kindly skill in the past. In any case the laird and his lady wished it, and they could do no wrong.

Next morning the Drummonds left at crack of dawn. The lady would stay in Edinburgh with friends while the laird, with the rest of the gentry, escorted King and court to the boundary of Midlothian. Then he would rejoin his wife and they would spend the sabbath in the city, not returning home until Monday. The arrangements had been made weeks ago. It could not be varied for two young nobodies like us.

Even so, it was just like our hostess to be a little apologetic in view of Barbary's bereavement. 'But you will not be lonely, I am sure. Robert will stay until we come back.' Again that thoughtful smile flickered at the corners of her mouth.

We rose early and dutifully, to bid them a respectful goodbye. They trotted away down the road with their personal servants riding behind.

And, sadly, we were destined never to see them again.

We had our dinner with the servants. We should have felt foolish eating by ourselves like guests of quality. Afterwards, Barbary said with a sigh, 'I must face it.'

'What must you face?'

'The cave. I can't live there by myself.'

'Of course not! The lady wouldn't let you. A young girl. When they come home—'

'But I'd better go back and clear the place. The sooner the better. It won't get easier. Gran had few enough possessions, but I cannot leave them. I must brace myself and go down there once more. Will you come with me?'

'Do you imagine I'd let you go alone?'

So we went down, out of the midday sunshine, into the gold-spangled shadows. Snapper trotted at our heels, cheering up visibly as we returned to the world with which he was familiar. He had been woebegone and uneasy during the last few days.

The cave was dank and chilly. The fire had been dead for days. I expect it had never gone out for years on end until Gran died. The cooking utensils were ancient. Under Barbary's instructions I threw them all, with other rubbish, into a nearby thicket.

She sorted her spare clothes with a mixture of amused disgust and wistful recollection of some kind giver. They were all cast-offs. Everything had had to be accepted with a show of gratitude. Many had given her a genuine thrill of delight, a glimpse of another world she would never know.

Life in the glen, she said, had never required much

171

attention to the changes of fashion. She sorted out one or two favourite garments, clean shifts and stockings and aprons, a white hood ('the right colour for a servant,' she said grimly), a shawl, a kerchief, pattens for walking on muddy days . . . 'These will do for the present. Later, with any luck . . .' She did not finish, but there was a light in her eyes. She was getting ready to face the future.

She went carefully over her grandmother's mysterious array of medicaments. She held things up to the light outside. She would stick a cautious fingertip into some ointment or liquid, identifying it on her tongue, sometimes with a comical grimace. No Latin labels here, I thought, remembering poor old Lownes.

She set aside five or six preparations. 'I know about *these*,' she said confidently. They were safe herbal cures for various aches and pains and suchlike homely afflictions. 'I've been glad enough of these myself, before now,' she admitted. 'I'll keep them.'

'And the others?'

She shook her head. 'I don't know. In Gran's hands they may have done a power of good. But some—' Again she made a face. 'They could work violently. They could be dangerous.' She shrugged her shoulders. 'Into the river, I think.'

I took them down and disposed of them. She made a bundle of what she would take away. 'Stupid!' she exclaimed suddenly. 'I'm forgetting the most important thing.'

'What's that?'

'Some folk paid her in coin. You did yourself. She had a place for it, though I was never allowed to touch it. It won't be much, but there's no sense in leaving it here.'

She walked into the furthest recesses of the cavern, stooped in the gloom and groped along the wall of rock. I heard a clink of coins.

'Found it?'

'Yes.' There were more clinks. 'Quite a lot. Come and lend me a hand.'

There were little heaps of coins along a ledge. We carried them out and spread them over the flat slab in the daylight. Most, as we expected, were of low value, like those I had once contributed myself. But there was a fair amount of silver, once or twice even the gleam of gold.

Gran's patients had not all been simple labouring folk. I thought of the merchant's wife at Burntisland, the gentry who put more faith in her than in physicians and apothecaries. Maybe the Drummonds themselves.

Barbary gathered the money carefully in a cloth bag. I was glad to know that, like me, she now had a little money of her own with which to start a new life.

Just then Snapper growled. For the second time on that very spot, at the cave mouth, we were startled by the voice of Guthrie.

'They said you'd gone for a walk. I guessed you might be here. The most dangerous place on earth you could be!'

Fifteen

We stepped out to meet him. Amazed. He was the last man to exaggerate.

'What do you mean?' Barbary demanded.

'They'll be here in a matter of hours. Looking for you!'

'Who?'

'A whole pack of them from Burntisland. And plenty of others will join them in Leith. Both sides of the water, folk are in a ferment. Have you never seen a witch hunt?' His tone was grim. 'I have. And never want to again. Ever.'

'Witch hunt?' I said. 'Mother Hume never harmed a soul. And she's dead now, anyway.'

His answer made my blood run cold. 'I don't mean Mother Hume. It's Barbary they'll be coming for.'

We both cried out incredulously.

He went on, heavily, 'Everyone's saying the ferry was sunk by witchcraft. That sudden storm—'

'That's always the cry,' I said scornfully.

I had heard that long ago, when King James's Danish princess came over to marry him, they had blamed witches for the storm which nearly wrecked her vessel. Freak storms were often attributed to evil spells.

'How do *I* come into it?' faltered Barbary. She had gone deathly pale.

'There's talk about a young woman standing on the quayside at Burntisland. She was heard putting a curse on the ferry.'

She laughed, but nervously. 'I did curse the ferryman, true. I was wild because he would not let me go aboard.'

It came back to me. How she had mocked the vessel's name. Said it should be the *Curse of Burntisland*, not the *Blessing*. Someone had remembered that angry shout and twisted its meaning.

'But they took me in the end,' she went on. 'And I nearly drowned when she turned over! If I was a witch why would I curse the ship I wanted to sail in?'

'You didn't drown, though,' he pointed out

176

patiently, 'and they reckon that supports the story. A witch *doesn't* drown. Of all the persons on board only two are known to have escaped alive. And one fits the description of the young woman who was heard uttering the curse.'

Now I understood the odd look given Barbary by the disagreeable man on the craft which picked us up.

That beautiful hair of hers, I thought – that was the real curse. It made it so easy to identify her. Worse still, in many people's minds red hair was the sign of a witch. Once the gossip spread someone must have remembered that Mother Hume, the wise woman of Hawthornden, had a red-haired assistant.

Everything hung together with a dreadful neatness. I recalled my grandfather's text: 'Thou shalt not suffer a witch to live.' His refusal to distinguish between a benevolent white witch and a wicked black one.

'I came to warn you,' Guthrie persisted. 'We must get you away from here. At once.'

'Where can I go?' She was really shaken now. 'Who can I turn to? The laird is away till Monday. *He* would stop them—'

'He would try. I don't know that he could. They'll be a raging mob. Those ferrymen have left widows and orphans. They had friends and kin. And there are plenty of other people who go mad at the mere word "witch".' I thought of the godly ministers of the kirk like my grandfather. 'If the laird tried to hide you away at Hawthornden,' said Guthrie, 'he'd very like have his house burnt about his ears!'

'That must not happen, Mr Guthrie,' she said. 'You're right. I must go. But where?'

I gripped her arm. 'Yes,' I challenged him, '*where?*'

'God knows! I'm known to be her friend. My farm is one of the first places they'd turn to.'

'So I must not be there. You must not come to harm on my account,' she said firmly. 'You must be able to throw open your door and bid them search. I shall get out of this parish, out of this district if possible. Only tell me where—'

'If only I could!' he groaned. He turned to me. 'Believe me, lad, once the hunt is on, there'll be no corner of Scotland where she'll be safe.' He seemed in utter despair.

It was my heart, not my head, that found the answer.

'In that case she had better come to England. I'll take her there.' In the stress of the situation I sounded more confident than I felt soon afterwards.

'It might be best.' He seemed at once dubious and relieved. 'I scarce know what to say, what to advise.'

I looked very straight into her eyes. '*You* must decide. We haven't much time. Will you come with me?'

Her eyes answered mine, and she nodded.

Guthrie promised to do all he could to set the hunt on the wrong scent. We had better not go back to the big house. We must leave behind our few possessions there. I pressed my hand to my belt and took comfort from the hard bulges of cash. Now Barbary had money too. I guessed we could pay our way to London.

'Will you take the laird aside and explain to him,' I asked, 'when he comes back on Monday?'

'I will, lad. He will understand.'

'And I will write to him when we are safe in London.'

'Our warmest thanks to him and to the lady,' said Barbary. 'I shall never forget how kind they have been.'

I shook his hand, she kissed him and we set off up the glen. There was no question of going back to see my grandparents. We should have walked straight into disaster at Leith. We must be well into the

179

Pentlands before dusk. Snapper padded softly at our heels. I had my doubts, because of his age, but we could not have left him behind. Barbary had lost so much, I could not ask her to give up her dog. I only hoped that he would not attract notice and hinder our escape.

That first night we found shelter in an empty shepherd's hut. We gathered armfuls of bracken to soften the earthen floor. Snapper stretched himself thankfully at Barbary's feet.

'He's even more exhausted than we are,' I said.

She leaned forward and stroked him. 'He's *so* old. I remember him when he was small. Dear, faithful Snapper.'

I wondered how he would take to London – if he ever got there. He did not get there. A few days later, sadly, we laid him to rest in a shallow grave we had scraped out in a Northumbrian wood.

But on that first evening we were making optimistic plans. Our panic was over. We had put a good few miles between us and Hawthornden. Except for calling at a tavern to buy some food – when Barbary had prudently stayed outside – we had left few clues. All too soon the story of the shipwreck and the witch's curse would spread through the credulous

180

countryside, but the Burntisland men and their Leith supporters were unlikely to get further than Hawthornden tonight.

'We must keep going,' I said, 'and avoid villages as far as we can. Once we're in England we'll be much safer. We'll get on to the Great North Road. We can lose ourselves among all those people travelling to and fro. We have money, we can buy proper meals, we can sleep somewhere better than this.'

She laughed. 'Remember, I have spent the last ten years in a cave.'

I licked my dry lips and took the plunge. 'Another thing, Barbary—'

'Yes? How serious you sound!'

'We must keep up a brother-and-sister pretence. We . . . may not find it easy.'

'We don't look much alike.'

'That's not the difficulty and well you know it. We must face facts. We're not children any longer.'

'You've noticed that?' She liked to tease me.

But I wasn't going to be put off. 'You must trust me. You know you can trust me?' I said earnestly. 'You understand?'

She understood all right. 'Yes, Rob.' She too was suddenly serious.

'You know how I feel about you?'

Her only answer was to press my hand.

I stumbled on. 'But I'll never . . . *do* anything. We *mustn't*, Bar.'

'I made my own resolutions,' she said, 'long ago. When my mother died and I was told what had happened to her, I was determined to have a better life than she'd had. May I tell you about her? I think now's the time.'

So I let her, though I had heard the whole tragic story from the Drummonds. I sensed that she was ready now to tell me about it, and passionately anxious to do so.

'So you see,' she ended, 'when someday *I* have a child – and please God I will – I mean everything to be different.'

I think I knew her even better after hearing all this in her own words.

'When we get to London,' I said, 'I shall hope to get men's parts – and a man's wage with them. And after that, soon, to become a sharer in the company. *I* can be determined, just as you can. *I* mean to make my way in the playhouse.'

'And you will, Rob. I know you will.'

'And *then*—' I pulled myself up. I was getting rather

intense. Which was best avoided in our present circumstances. Time to strike a lighter note. 'There's an old actor in our company,' I said. 'Plays the clowns and suchlike parts. He gave me what he said was the wisest motto for any young man.'

'Which was?'

I quoted the couplet. 'Till you're sure you'll earn your bread, Ask no wench to share her bed.'

'*Robert!*' she rocked with laughter. 'I'll see you keep to that!' But she turned and kissed me full on the lips, and I knew that when the time came all would be well, very well.

When we reached London my hopes of work were justified. Our manager listened with interest to my account of the masque at Welbeck and my subsequent adventures.

'You know, Rob,' he said, 'this journey was well worth making. It's matured you. You went away as a boy, and you've come back—' He paused and smiled. 'Well, let's just say I'd like to try you in a man's part.'

He did, and seemed satisfied. After a while, when we revived some of Shakespeare's tragedies, I was given my chance as Romeo. I could imagine Barbary's catlike smile as she watched. She was selling oranges in the audience.

'I near burst my bodice, holding in my laughter,' she confessed afterwards, 'to see you making passionate love to that padded boy!' But she had controlled herself because, she assured me, the rest of the people were rapt, and she did not want to lose her job as an orange-seller.

She was doing that because she had insisted on paying my mother for her keep until she lawfully became a member of the family. Which she soon did, now that I could earn the daily bread for two – or more – and we were free to go looking for a place of our own. And life really began.

Author's Note

After finishing an historical novel one often wonders how much was fact and how much fiction. This story closely follows, from the performance at Welbeck Abbey to the crossing of the Firth of Forth, the King's coronation journey to Scotland in 1633 as detailed by the Privy Council and other documents. Many characters are as real as Charles the First himself. A handwritten acting copy of Ben Jonson's *Masque at Welbeck*, preserving his own marginal notes on stage directions and costumes, survives as Harley MS 4955 in that famous collection of manuscripts. The annual Hawthornden Prize for imaginative literature still commemorates the laird of that place. The Earl (later Duke) of Newcastle was no less real: my own *Portrait of a Cavalier* is his biography. Even poor Mr Lownes, the apothecary, and his cart, which never got back to the Tower of London, still figure in the official records. The remedies used by white witches are taken from those known to have been prescribed, though they are not necessarily recommended to modern readers for either head pains or hangovers. In the following year, according to the Calendar of State Papers for 16 May, 1634, a trial of nineteen witches was held in Lancashire, when the women were sentenced to death for causing that very same storm which occurred in Scotland the previous July.

G.T.

Bath 1994

A WATERY GRAVE
A Karen Cady Mystery

Penny Kline

*The body of a young girl pulled from a reservoir.
An unsolved crime. One suspect.*

Flame-haired Karen Cady, hoping to follow
in her father's private detective footsteps,
thinks she can solve the mystery. *Someone* must
know who killed Natalie Stevens – and why.

An unexplained headline in a newspaper. A
case that has remained unsolved for six
months. A secret that someone is prepared
to kill to keep . . .

FERAL KID

Libby Hathorn

Robbie, homeless, caught up in a crime he wants no part of . . . Iris, an old lady he mugs in a city park . . .

Their chance meeting brings about an unlikely friendship. A friendship that offers both a new future.

But can life really change for the better?

'I found this fascinating. It looks at homelessness from a different angle to *Stone Cold*, and is a great deal more optimistic, without underplaying society's indifference'
ROBERT SWINDELLS

WHEN THE SNOW FALLS

Michael Lawrence

Do we each have a double – someone whose life mirrors ours?

There was a fifty-fifty chance that she would survive. But Rob's mother died.

Then the snow falls . . .

And Rob meets Bobby.
A girl who lives in a house just like his.
A girl who looks just like him.
A girl whose mother is still alive.

And Rob is shown how life might have been . . .

THE GHOST MESSENGERS

Roberts Swindells

Haunted by the ghosts of her grandfather and his wartime bomber crew, Meg tries to make sense of their strange and puzzling messages. These visitations disturb her sleep and her schoolwork, and are somehow intensified by the conservation work in the local woodland.

Can Meg decipher the messages before it's too late?

'This well-plotted book . . . proceeds to a genuinely exciting climax.'

Junior Bookshelf

A CANDLE IN THE DARK

Robert Swindells

Sent to work down the mines as a pit-brat,
Jimmy Booth enters a harsh and violent world
from which there seems to be no escape.
Then he discovers the secret of Rawdon Pit,
a dangerous secret that could change his life
– or end it.

ORDER FORM

0 340 32098 2	Candle in the Dark *Robert Swindells*	£3.50	❏
0 340 64672 1	The Ghost Messengers *Robert Swindells*	£3.50	❏
0 340 62671 2	When The Snow Falls *Michael Lawrence*	£3.50	❏
0 340 65124 5	Feral Kid *Libby Hathorn*	£3.50	❏
0 340 64847 3	A Watery Grave *Penny Kline*	£3.50	❏

All Hodder Children's books are available at your local bookshop or newsagent, or can be ordered direct from the publisher. Just tick the titles you want and fill in the form below. Prices and availability subject to change without notice.

Hodder Children's Books, Cash Sales Department, Bookpoint, 39 Milton Park, Abingdon, OXON, OX14 4TD, UK. If you have a credit card you may order by telephone – (01235) 831700.

Please enclose a cheque or postal order made payable to Bookpoint Ltd to the value of the cover price and allow the following for postage and packing:
UK & BFPO – £1.00 for the first book, 50p for the second book, and 30p for each additional book ordered up to a maximum charge of £3.00.
OVERSEAS & EIRE – £2.00 for the first book, £1.00 for the second book, and 50p for each additional book.

Name..

Address..

....

....
If you would prefer to pay by credit card, please complete:
Please debit my Visa/Access/Diner's Card/American Express (delete as applicable) card no:

Signature..

Expiry Date..